F

10

10

7

Nevada Hawk

The long trail ended at Castle Rock in New Mexico Territory. Nevada found the man who had murdered his wife and killed him as he'd planned for over a year. He had never thought beyond the moment of vengeance until now. What was the next step?

A man of Nevada's talents with a gun was always in demand. He didn't care what type of work he took on, or how dangerous. Life – his own that is – no longer mattered much any more. Or did it?

He would breathe plenty of gunsmoke before he found the answer.

Nevada Hawk

Hank J. Kirby

A Black Horse Western

ROBERT HALE · LONDON

© Hank J. Kirby 2006
First published in Great Britain 2006

ISBN-10: 0-7090-8094-8
ISBN-13: 978-0-7090-8094-7

Robert Hale Limited
Clerkenwell House
Clerkenwell Green
London EC1R 0HT

Typeset by
Derek Doyle & Associates, Shaw Heath
Printed and bound in Great Britain by
Antony Rowe Limited, Wiltshire

CHAPTER 1

NOTCH FIVE

Already six weeks of the second summer of the manhunt had passed when he rode into Castle Rock.

It had started during midsummer the year before, in Arizona. He had hunted the men all through autumn, the bleakness of winter – almost died in a blizzard in Utah – and in late spring had picked up the sign that had eventually led him here to this scattered adobe town that was typical of this part of northern New Mexico. Deep down in his gut he felt that the long trail of vengeance would finally end here.

There were four notches already in the cedar butt of his gun. Notch five was overdue, but now coming up. . . . *And the day after he carved in notch five. . . ? He'd worry about that when it happened. And all the days after that. . . . Later! Later! Too much else to think about right now. . . .*

For the present, he was content to set his trail-

5

weary chestnut down from the mesa that gave the town its name. He was a patient man.

As he drew closer, the glare from the white buildings made his lead-coloured eyes squint down. He let the chestnut make its own way, tugged at the lead rope attached to the bridle of the just-as-weary buckskin trailing behind. *Clip-clop, clip-clop.* For some reason he thought of it as a satisfying sound, taking him to his goal, but he was really too damn tired to figure out why. He yawned until his jaw hinges creaked, scrubbed a rough hand down his stubbled face. He'd need food and sleep, not to mention a hot bath in plenty of soapy water before starting to look for his quarry. No sense in going after a man like Ketchum, half-starved and barely able to keep his eyes open.

There were better ways for a man to commit suicide if he had that kind of thing in mind. Don't make a joke out of it! It's not all that long ago since the prospect of ending it all seemed to hold its attractions. . . .

He came to a rooming-house that backed on to the creek and stopped there, paying a raggedy-pants kid a nickel to watch his horses enjoy the muddy shallows, while he scrubbed the grime of a thousand miles of hard trails from his lean body. 'Let 'em graze on the bank till I come for 'em,' he instructed, heading for the nearby bath-house.

Afterwards, he ordered a meal and the young half-Indian girl who delivered the tray seemed willing to include herself in the deal. He smiled, shook his head, pushing wet hair back off his scarred forehead.

'Ask me again tomorrow,' he stalled and she pouted, but smiled coquettishly as she went out.

He had a change of clothes in his battered saddle-bags, faded from much washing and travelling but mostly presentable. With a full belly swelled some more by six cups of decent coffee, he sat on the edge of the lumpy bed, took his Colt apart and cleaned it thoroughly, using the last of his gun oil. He took each weathered cartridge from the loops in his belt and rubbed up every single one with the oily cloth. He didn't aim for any compacted alkali dust around the rim to cause a misfire or clog his cylinder's slow movement as it turned after each shot.

Yeah – there would be more than one shot, when he faced down Ketchum. He'd make damn sure of that.

The boy had done as ordered and the big stranger led both his horses, still wet from the creek, to the livery. The hostler wanted payment in advance, not much liking what he saw of this gun-hung stranger with the week-old beard stubble and the wrinkled old clothes. But the man managed to rake up enough and said:

'Looking for a feller. Big as me, maybe heavier. Red hair, but not carrot-bright. Axeblade nose that leans to the left, and he might have a nick out of one ear-lobe – the left one.'

The hostler was interested but tried to appear casual, leaning on the long handle of his hayfork. 'Seem to have this feller's description down pat. What's his name?'

'Wouldn't help. He's likely changed it. . . . You seen him?'

The hostler pursed his lips, shook his head. 'Mebbe seen fellers somethin' like that driftin' through, but . . .' He shrugged again. 'Dunno your man. Sorry.'

The stranger didn't believe him. Something had moved in the hostler's eyes when he had mentioned the crooked nose and the notched ear-lobe.

'No one like that come to town lately and stayed. . . ? Set up in some kinda business, maybe. . . ?'

'I'd know if that was the case.'

'Yeah – but would you tell me?'

The hostler was no midget, sized up the stranger but backed off from the smart-ass remark that almost fell from the tip of his tongue. *This* hombre *looked mighty dangerous. . . .*

'Well, course I would! I mean, be no skin off my nose. Er – is this feller wanted for somethin'? Mebbe there's some kinda re-ward?'

The stranger got it then and smiled slightly. 'Not right now, but I'd remember anyone who helped me find him before I quit town.'

'Hmmmm. Well, if I do think of somethin' I'll let you know. You got a name?'

'Nevada'll do.' The stranger started to walk back down the aisle.

'Where can I find you. . . ?'

Nevada didn't answer, went out through the big double doors into the sunlight and turned left towards the boardwalk and the business area.

The hostler leaned the hayfork against the wall, stalled the stranger's horses and took off his stained leather apron. He was humming quietly to himself when he went out the small side door towards the rear, next to the cubicle he used as an office. He hurried around the biggest corral where he ran his hire mounts and those horses that belonged to townsfolk who had nowhere to keep them at their own place.

He crossed the wooden bridge over the creek, nodded 'howdy' to a couple of men lounging outside a barber's and hurried on down to the end of the block, crossed an alley and turned into the building on the corner.

From where he had been lounging in the doorway of a store, Nevada could just make out the name on the shingle swinging on a thin-linked chain above the door the livery man entered.

James Corey – Land Agent

He nodded to himself, face grim, unconsciously eased the heavy, newly oiled Colt in the holster.

Now, all he had to do was get a good look at Mr James Corey and, if his hunch was right, he would have Linus Ketchum in his sights before sundown.

Corey was a heavy man, heavier than the stranger who had described him to the hostler. His hair was a darker shade of red; maybe some folk would call it auburn. His moustache was a little lighter and was thick enough to droop over his upper lip. He sat back in his chair now and scratched idly at the mangled lobe of his left ear, an old, involuntary habit.

'Nevada, you say?' he asked the hostler, arching his thin eyebrows. Corey shook his head. 'Don't know him. Why did you think you had to tell me?'

'Described you to a T – 'cept for the moustache.' The livery man moved his straw-and-manure-covered boots restlessly.'You been doin' real well with the land deals since you opened this office here, Mr Corey. Thought you might . . . appreciate . . . knowin' someone was lookin' for you. Tough-lookin' someone. . . .'

Bleak, suspicious eyes raked the hostler, made the man more uneasy than ever. 'Could be just someone who wants to settle here, looking for land, maybe.'

The hostler smiled crookedly.'He didn't ask for a land agent. I think he's lookin' for more than that.'

'What, for instance?'

The livery man didn't want to answer, not with those cold eyes boring into him. *Maybe he'd said enough – or too much – already.* He licked his lips, shrugged. 'I . . . I just thought you'd wanna know. Guess I'll be goin' now, Mr Corey.'

'Thanks for dropping by, Asa. But next time clean your damn boots before you come into my office.'

Asa Poole nodded jerkily and went out, surprised to find how much he was sweating.

Corey stood and leaned out his office's side-window, whistling quietly to a wide-shouldered man who was sitting on the stoop of the storeshed out back, idly smoking. When the man looked up, sunlight washing over a rugged, moon face, Corey gestured with a jerk of his head. The big man, Lew Abbott, stood instantly and hurried across the yard.

He entered the office looking expectant, his checkered shirt dark under the armpits, a cardboard tobacco-sack tag on a string hanging from the pocket.

'You want me, chief?'

Corey was seated at his desk again now, toying with a pencil. He glanced at Abbott and nodded gently.

'I think that man I told you about has just arrived in town. Calling himself Nevada again and asking about me.'

'The one you figured's been followin' you?'

Corey nodded again, looking perplexed. 'I've heard about him over the past six months, somewhere along my back-trail, always describing me. Never asking for me by name.'

'Which name would that be?' As soon as he spoke, Abbott wished he had kept his mouth shut. Trying to ignore the bleak look, he cleared his throat, said: 'You always say you dunno him.'

'I don't. I've heard him called Nevada, sometimes Hawk, but the names mean nothing to me, nor does his description. Take a look around town, see if you can find him, maybe buy him a drink, and ask a few questions.' He stood and reached for the clean, fawn Stetson with the dent in the high crown, set it on his head, then took a Smith & Wesson double-action Russian model revolver from a desk drawer and placed it in a holster under his left arm. As he straightened his coat, hiding the gun rig, Abbott said:

'Want me to walk you home?'

'No, I'll drive the buggy. You find this Nevada

and . . .' He paused and then his moustache straightened as he tightened his mouth. '*Yes, damnit!* It's time to find out what the hell he wants with me! I'm fed up hearing about him.'

Abbott lifted thick black eyebrows. 'Want me to end it once and for all?'

Corey hesitated. 'If you have to. Anything to get him off my back. He's been there long enough.'

And it's making you mighty jumpy, Lew Abbott thought as he opened the office door for his boss, frowning slightly as the man passed through on to the boardwalk.

Well, he'd known for a long time that Corey was paying him fighting pay – now it seemed it was time for him to start earning it.

Which was OK with Abbott: it was about time he had a chance to use the twin Colts in the polished *buscadero* rig he wore about his thick middle.

But he was too eager. When he found the man having a beer in the saloon – and gathering information about 'Corey' in his own quiet way – Abbott felt riled and gave away more than he intended right from the start.

Impatient, thirsty and hot, he sidled up alongside Nevada and without preamble said sharply:

'Hear you're lookin' for Mr Corey. I want to know why. And you better have a good reason!'

Nevada turned his head slowly and looked Abbott over. He saw a typical flash gunman, the bodyguard type who did a lot of swaggering, knowing he had power backing him.

'Man I'm looking for is named Ketchum. I've described him. Does your Corey sound like the man I want?'

'Listen, you just quit botherin' Mr Corey. *That's* his name and he don't need any grief from some drifter.'

'Got a guilty conscience, has he?'

Lew Abbott frowned. 'You're pushin' this! You *want* trouble!'

'No. Got all I need.'

'Well, you heed what I said or you'll have a heap more.' Abbott deliberately knocked over Nevada's beer-glass, spilling its contents, forcing the drifter to jump back. Lew grinned tightly. 'See how quick things can change?'

Nevada nodded, seeing the splashes of beer down his faded trousers. Without looking up he crashed his right fist against the side of Abbott's jaw and sent him staggering and floundering half-way down the bar. Other drinkers scattered and those at tables looked up, suddenly interested.

Abbott steadied, shook his head, rubbing his aching jaw. His eyes blazed and while his left hand massaged his face, his right dipped towards the butt of his other sixgun.

He froze, staring down the barrel of Nevada's Colt which had appeared in the big man's fist, hammer cocked. The lead-coloured eyes were flat and steady.

'How'd you ever get a job guarding Ketchum? I could've put three bullets in you before your got your gun clear of leather. . . .' He jerked his head towards the batwings. 'Git. Go tell Ketchum I'll see him in my own good time.'

13

The room was silent, except for Abbott's heavy breathing. He opened his right hand, raised it up from his side. His face was flushed, eyes very wary. He continued to stare at Nevada for a moment or two longer, then heeled sharply and strode out of the bar. Nevada holstered his gun and turned to the barkeep.

'Gimme another beer. You can put it on that feller's tab.'

'Whatever you say, mister.'

The 'keep's hands trembled slightly as he drew a frothing beer and set it before Nevada, who nodded his thanks.

During his short visit to the saloon Nevada had learned that the man who called himself James Corey had arrived in Castle Rock five months ago, bought out the local land agent and set himself up in business.

A month later he had courted and married a well-heeled widow named Amelia Marsden. They had built a large house on a knoll on the south side of town, the 'better' side, some folk liked to say.

Nevada had had a couple of good looks at 'Corey' and there was no doubt in his mind that he was the man he wanted. The moustache did little to hide his features with their trade-mark battered nose and mangled ear-lobe. This was Linus Ketchum, all right, and it was now time to finish the job he had started more than a year ago.

So he waited for dark, then went out to the knoll south of Castle Creek, and saw that the land agent's house was a grand affair. Double-storeyed, with pillared porch, neat gardens – a stand-out in this town, but obviously meant for permanancy as far as Ketchun was concerned.

Well, it could well be a permanent memorial, allowed Nevada silently, as he made his way through bushes towards the building where lights showed at tall windows.

A permanent black spot on the landscape.

He shucked the half-gallon bottle of coal-oil he had bought out of the old flour sack and began to work the cork out of the neck, just loosening it, not removing it.

Yet.

CHAPTER 2

GUNHAWK

It wasn't often that Amelia Corey answered the front door herself, but tonight happened to be the staff's night off – except for the Mexican cookwoman and her daughter.

Vaguely irritated at having the evening meal interrupted, yet a little relieved for the excuse to leave her husband's edginess and snappy mood, she hurried down the hall and unlocked the big heavy carved door: imported mahogany from Asia.

She saw a big untidy-looking man standing there, unshaven, clothes faded and wrinkled and for a moment some of the words her husband had been bandying about over the meal came to mind:

'. . . Saddle tramp in looks, but tough. Leastways he dropped Lew Abbott, who's no ballet dancer. . . . Asked for me by describing me! Hell, I don't know him, yet he described me like – like I could be his brother. . . .'

Was this that man? Amelia wondered now. She was a smallish woman in her mid-thirties, whose health was mostly poorly. But there was iron in that hard-angled jaw that somehow enhanced the other soft, feminine lines, giving them unexpected strength. Her cool gaze looked him up and down in a flash and her full mouth tightened slightly as she said in clipped tones: 'There is absolutely no need for you to try to knock my front door down, young man!'

'Just trying to get your attention, ma'am,' Nevada said, touching a hand to his battered hatbrim.

'Well, you have it. What do you want?'

'Just passing and thought you'd like to know the rear of your house is on fire.'

She blinked, going very still, unsure that she had heard him right. 'House. . . ? On – fire. . . ?'

'Yes'm. Got a pretty good hold I'd reckon. Breeze is blowing crosswise right now which is likely why you never smelled the smoke. If you got any valuables you'd be as well to grab 'em quick and get out of danger. You and anyone else in the house.'

Amelia drew herself up to her full height of five feet three inches. 'Young man, if you think this is amusing, I have to warn you that my husband is a man of note in this community and—'

There was the sound of breaking glass somewhere behind her and she whirled – in time to see flames licking in through a broken rear window at the far end of the hallway. A woman's scream of alarm came from the kitchen area.

'Oh my goodness!' Amelia's hand flew to her mouth, her eyes widening. A startled Jim Corey came bursting out of the dining-room. 'What in the hell? God almighty, we're on fire!'

'Spotted it as I was walking by. Just telling your wife about it right now, Mr – Ketchum.'

'Corey' spun towards the front door where Amelia seemed ready to swoon, certainly frozen in shock and possibly fear. The land agent's face went white and he grabbed at the wall, eyes hardening as he saw Nevada.

'By God! You're – him! The one's been dogging me all these months!'

'One year, eleven days and near enough to nineteen hours, Ketchum,' Nevada answered tightly.

Amelia looked from one man to the other and Corey, obviously unarmed, backed up against the wall, still staring.

Nevada touched a hand to his hatbrim again and nodded in Amelia's direction. 'You'd best concentrate on trying to save your fine house. You and me can continue this conversation later, Ketchum.'

'Who the hell are you?' shouted Ketchum as Nevada turned and walked back down the path, the way lit up by the roaring flames, which were climbing up and over the roof by now, more glass breaking, the Mexican women shouting wildly.

'Who is that man?' he heard Amelia screaming above the roar and crackle of the fire. 'Why did he call you 'Ketchum'. . . ?'

Nevada paused by the gate, smiling crookedly. 'Yeah. Try to explain that, Ketchum!' The firelight played on the hard planes of his now expressionless face as he watched the mansion become engulfed in flames. He heard the shouts of folk running up the hill from town, coughed once as a swirl of choking smoke rampaged past him.

'Judas priest! What happened?' a townsman yelled.

'Ya blind, Kerry? You think that's a barbecue sizzlin' an' roarin' away there?'

'The fire pump'll never lift water up the hill from the crick!'

'Nah, you're right there. She's a goner.'

'Hope it singes Amelia's britches – she needs takin' down a peg or two.'

'Mebbe it's her britches need takin' down!'

There was ribald laughter as, unnoticed in the jostling crowd, Nevada walked back to town and made his way to his rooming-house by the creek.

The hill where Ketchum's house was stood out like a giant Roman candle. Then an eruption of sparks and hurtling red stars exploded across the night sky.

'There goes the roof!' someone yelled.

Nevada felt his belly tighten as he made his way to the door of the rooming-house.

How come he didn't feel more . . . satisfied?

There was only a kind of deadness in him now, and it was slowly spreading all through his body. He didn't even bother to take off his boots as he lay down on the narrow bed. His sixgun was ready to hand on a chair where he could reach it easily. He closed his eyes but he knew sleep would not come to him easily this night.

Maybe it was because it wasn't over yet – not by a long way.

Ketchum didn't wait till daylight to square up to the man who had burned his mansion to the ground.

He did not come in person, but he sent two men to the narrow balcony outside Nevada's room. Their shadows showed on the torn brown-paper blind and the interruption to moonlight across his face made Nevada open his eyes.

Glass broke as the twin barrels of a heavy Greener smashed into the room and blasted in flame-stabbing thunder that made the room tremble.

By that time Nevada was on the floor, sixgun in hand, blazing in rapid fire. The remains of the glass shattered and a man yelled, another screamed. A body fell into the room, tearing loose the smouldering brown-paper blind, giving him a glimpse of the screaming man still out there, doubled over, holding his belly.

Nevada put another shot into him and rolled across the floor as the door was kicked in and Lew Abbott bounded in, crouching, his Colt throwing daggers of flame into the semi-dark room as he hunted Nevada.

The drifter was lying hard up against the wall under the window now, heard his gun hammer fall on an empty shell even as he tried to kick free of the body of the shotgun man who had fallen through the window. The body jerked as one of Abbott's bullets found a home, and Nevada felt swiftly, located the dead man's Colt and dragged it free of leather.

Lew sidled into the room, searching still for

Nevada's dark shape. He heard the dead man's Colt whisper from leather, saw a dull reflection of light from the metal and spun that way, shooting. Nevada fired at the same time, twice. Lew Abbott grunted, staggered back into the door where it was folded back against the wall. He tried to bring the smoking gun up but Nevada nailed him with one last shot and Abbott crumpled noisily to the floor, unmoving.

Ears ringing, coughing in the thick pall of gunsmoke, Nevada hunched down in a dark corner and hurriedly reloaded his own Colt. By then, folk in the rooming-house were finding enough courage to come slinking up to the door and someone asked tentatively:

'Anyone still alive in there. . . ?'

A man came running up the hill to where Sheriff Lang Hewitt was standing looking at the smouldering ruins, scratching his jaw thoughtfully. Panting, the messenger said:

'Sheriff! Best come. Been a shootin' at the Creekside roomin'-house. That big stranger just killed three men!' He glanced at the grey-faced Ketchum standing beside his wife, whose expensive dress was no longer expensive, hung from her rather full figure in torn ribbons. Her face was begrimed, with tear-tracks meandering through the smuts. 'One of the dead men was Lew Abbott, Mr Corey.'

Ketchum swore softly, ignoring the poke in the ribs given him by his wife. He looked hard at the sheriff. 'Well? Why you just standing there, Lang? Go arrest the son of a bitch!'

21

Hewitt, a gangling man in his forties, scratched at his lantern jaw and drawled, 'Well, now, Mr Corey, would seem to me like there's somethin' more to this than meets the eye.'

'The hell're you talking about? Aah, what am I doing standing here trying to talk sense into a drunk!'

'James, just what *is* happening?' asked Amelia bewilderedly, with a hard edge to her query. 'First this drifter sets fire to our house, warns us in time so we can get out safely, and now he's killed three men in a gunfight – one of them Lew Abbott who you've always claimed was the best gunfighter north of the Rio Grande.'

'The man's got me mixed up with someone else. I-I'm not sticking around waiting for the maniac to put a bullet into me.' He grabbed the startled woman by the upper arms, looking down into her face. 'Amelia, I'm going to have to quit town for a few days. Just till this Nevada comes to his senses, or our brave sheriff finds enough guts to either throw him in jail or shoot him down.'

'Wh-what about me?'

'You'll be all right. It's me he wants.'

'But – where can you go. . . ?'

'I-I've been doing some business with the mines on the far side of the mesa – they're wanting to lease more land. I'll go stay out there for a little while. Harding has plenty of tough men on the payroll should this Nevada decide to come after me.' He stooped and kissed her lightly on the cheek. 'I'm sorry, my dear. . . . But it won't be for long.'

He turned to the frowning sheriff. 'Just try and earn the wage we pay you, for once, Lang! Get this maniac behind bars or shoot him down!'

'Damn you, James! Don't you leave me like this!'

He thrust Amelia away from him, turned and started to run down the hill towards town and the livery stables.

The messenger, bursting with news now after what he had just witnessed, started back down the slope to the saloon where he knew the men who had vainly fought the fire were gathering for a well-earned drink.

He was surprised to find Nevada there, sitting in a corner chair, alone at a table with a whiskey-bottle and shotglass before him. Even as he watched, the man poured two drinks one after the other, throwing them down his throat quickly.

'Mister, I was you I'd light a shuck. Reckon you done the town a favour killin' Lew Abbott and them two deadbeats he had tryin' to nail you through the window. But Sheriff Hewitt's on his way down here now. And Jim Corey's headin' for the livery, says he's quitting town till they throw you in jail – or shoot you.'

Nevada's eyes seemed a little out of focus and he frowned, staring, for a long moment, then he stood, hitched at his gunbelt and headed for the batwings. The smoke-smelling, ash-grimed drinkers watched him go, then swung their gazes back to the tensed messenger.

'Well come on! He's goin' to head off Corey at the livery! This trouble ain't over yet – whatever it is!'

There was a general rush now towards the saloon's exits.

Corey recklessly threw a double-eagle at Asa Poole and ordered him to saddle the fastest horse he had in his corrals – and to do it pronto. Asa was never a slouch when it came to earning easy money and he had a sleek, ripple-muscled sorrel saddled in almost nothing flat. He led it into the aisle were Corey paced nervously, checking his Smith & Wesson over and over. He holstered the gun as the hostler brought the horse to him, snatched the reins and turned towards the exit.

Then he froze.

There was a man standing right in the middle of the big double doorway, standing easy, arms loosely at his sides, feet a little spread. He was silhouetted against the lights of town and Ketchum-Corey saw the movement of a crowding bunch of men behind Nevada.

'Don't go yet, Ketchum. We ain't finished by a long sight.'

Linus Ketchum seemed to cave in slightly. He dropped the reins of the sorrel, staring at Nevada. Asa Poole sidled forward, led the sorrel into a stall out of danger – he was always a man who liked to protect his own property, especially if it was valuable.

'Who the hell are you?' demanded Ketchum, the shock fading now as he realized that this was the showdown and he couldn't avoid it. 'What the hell did I ever do to you?'

'Nothing. Not personally.'

The crowd was hushed and Ketchum frowned. 'Then what d'you want with me? Someone paying you to get me?'

Nevada shook his head. 'No. It's all my idea.'

'Christ! Then why?'

'Sabre Wells, Arizona. Just over a year ago.'

Ketchum frowned. There was a rising fear now behind his eyes, but he hardened his facial lines, scratched at his mangled ear-lobe briefly, then released a long breath.

'What about it?' He spoke in almost a whisper.

'The Tombstone stage – carrying payment for a shipment of gold and silver.' Nevada's voice was flat, emotionless. His deadly eyes never moved a fraction from Ketchum's face, the pale skin standing out against the smudge-marks. 'A gang of five scum-of-the-trails held up the stage. There was quite a payroll in that express box. But that didn't satisfy those mangy thieves! They had to go on a killing spree. They'd already shot the driver and shotgun guard, wounded a male passenger. They finished him off after making him run for the sagebrush with one leg dangling from a splintered bone and a few shreds of flesh.

'Must've been lots of fun for those snakes, driving him on. Then there were only two women passengers left. . . .'

'Goddlemighty!' someone breathed in the darkness behind Nevada, some townsman with enough imagination to see what was coming.

Ketchum hadn't moved. He was frozen, scarcely breathing, his eyes watering from the strain of trying

25

to hold Nevada's icy gaze.

'When you and your filthy bastards had finished with them, you still weren't content. You threw them into the stagecoach, nailed up the doors, then set it afire, with the team spooked and running flat out. . . . One of your men, called himself 'Danno', told me just before I killed him that the stage ran for almost half a mile before it crashed on to its side. He said you could hear every last scream those women made while the flames ate at 'em. . . .'

Ketchum still didn't move or speak. His nostrils were flared on his crooked nose above the ginger moustache and his chest heaved a little, but otherwise he was as still and as stiff as a rock carving.

'One of those women was my wife,' Nevada said flatly, hushed. 'She was on her way to the ranch I'd bought and gotten ready for her at Argenta. . . .'

After what seemed like a long silence but was, in reality, only seconds, there was a tight murmur from the men gathered behind Nevada. He didn't turn or move his deadly gaze from Ketchum.

'Best step back gents,' he said quietly, then addressed Ketchum again. 'I was gonna let your wife burn in that house on the hill, Ketchum, but I couldn't do it. . . . That doesn't mean I can't – and won't – kill you, though.'

'You got the wrong man,' Ketchum's voice was raspy, phlegmy as he finally got out some words. 'The wrong man!'

'No. I've had a year to get my facts right. I sold the ranch after I buried . . . what was left of Ellie. Used the money to buy me the best information. You're the rotten snake I want, Ketchum, and this is as far as you go. You're gonna die right here, right where you're standing now. You can go for your gun if you like, but it won't bother me none if you don't. You're still going to die.'

'You shoot me down in cold blood they'll hang you!' Desperation and a rising terror he had never known before made Ketchum's voice tremble.

Nevada's thin lips made a tight, crooked smile. 'You think I care about what happens to me? I've been a walking dead man since I first got word that my wife had been incinerated in that stagecoach.' Nevada made a calm gesture towards Ketchum's gun. 'Wanna make a try for it? Might as well. Just don't expect any special break. *C'mon!* It's time!'

Ketchum knew this was the moment when he *had* to make his play, *had* to, or he was certainly a dead man.

With a little whine that jumped up from somewhere deep inside him, Ketchum snatched at his Smith & Wesson Russian Model pistol.

He almost made it, was a lot faster than Nevada had figured.

But ultimately, it was way too late for Linus Ketchum.

He died before he hit the ground, his body torn and twisted by the hammering lead from Nevada's Colt that smashed into him. Ketchum was not a pretty sight when he spread out in the filth of the livery aisle, blood running from beneath him in several directions.

Nevada stood there, smoking pistol still in his

hand, face blank – no, *dead* was more like it – as he stared down at the man he had hunted all this time.

He was damned glad he'd killed Ketchum – *damned* glad – but how come he didn't feel . . . good? No surge of elation, no ringing bells of relief inside his head, no loosening of his gut that had been knotted solid for over a year now. . . ?

How come?

CHAPTER 3

LOCK-UP

Sheriff Hewitt wiped a kerchief down his sweat-beaded face and ran a tongue over his lips. He could almost taste the redeye he had stashed in the bottom drawer of his battered desk. But just knowing it was there, within reach, whenever he wanted it, would carry him through the next few minutes all right.

He was still begrimed from the fire – not that he had helped fight it, but he had made a token inspection of the smouldering, blackened ruins. It looked good to the watchers, though, as if he had been right on the ball, doing the job he was paid for.

Now he stood outside the barred door of the cell where Nevada sat on the edge of the bunk rolling a cigarette.

'I've been around guns and law for quite a spell, mister, but damned if I ever recollect hearin' about a gunfighter named Nevada.'

The prisoner looked up briefly as he licked his

cigarette paper and twisted up the slim cylinder. 'Nothing to hear. I'm no gunhawk.'

'You've just killed four men in my town!'

'They needed killing.'

'Beside the point. Lew Abbott was a hired gun. By all 'counts Corey – this one you keep callin' Ketchum – was no slowpoke neither.'

Nevada shook out his match and exhaled smoke, hitching around and putting his back against the wall, boots on the grey blanket of the hard, narrow bunk.

'I'm a cattleman, Sheriff. I was an Indian fighter for a time but that was done mostly with a rifle. I could handle a sixgun no better, no worse, than the average range ranny. But when I found out what had happened to my wife. . . .'

He stopped and Hewitt waited a while, then nodded. 'You put in some practice. Lots of practice.'

Nevada nodded briefly. 'I aimed to track down those bastards who'd killed Ellie, one by one. Just worked out that the leader was the last I found. I'd've killed him anywhere along the line I'd run into him, though.'

'You got a killer streak in you, Nevada. And what's your real name? Where you from?'

'Not Nevada. Dunno where I'm from. Some folk took me in when I was a shaver and they told me they got me from a mountain man who said he'd found me as the only survivor of a wagon train attacked by Indians along the Oregon Trail. These folk who raised me spent a deal of time in Nevada – they gave me a name, I guess, but I run off for some reason I don't recollect and next time someone asked me my name I said Nevada and it stuck.'

'Where's the "Hawk" come in?'

'Bid for a job as trail boss for a big cattle outfit and they said I needed two names for the contract. Folk often told me I had eyes like a hawk, so. . . .' He shrugged. Then he drew on his cigarette, watching the sheriff closely, seeing the long fingers drumming against the man's thighs. 'You mightn't've heard about me, Hewitt, but I know your name.'

The lawman tensed. 'Once it was . . . pretty well known.'

'Yeah. I spent a lot of time in Arizona. You tamed a few towns – Nogales, Tombstone, Tucson – and they say you left your mark on the Kansas trail towns before that.'

Hewitt squared his shoulders a little, but he had learned long ago that he couldn't live on old pride for ever. So he shrugged. 'I was a lot younger then.'

'You're not old now. Not old enough for a man like you to bury yourself in a hole like this.'

'Aw, it's not so bad. Big things'll happen to Castle Rock. Your friend Corey – Ketchum – saw that, got into the land-agency business, tied in with the mines on the other side of the mesa. There's plenty potential here.'

Nevada drew deeply on his cigarette. 'It ever comes to pass, they won't keep you as sheriff,' he said flatly and saw the hurt flare in the other's eyes before Hewitt worked up a little anger. But it was obvious that he had no stomach for arguing about his prowess – or lack of it now.

'Well, just mebbe I'll surprise a lot of folk!' Hewitt said weakly. 'Anyway, I don't have to stand here an' listen to you insult me.'

As the lawman turned away, Nevada said: 'What happens now?' He hadn't given Hewitt any resistance when he had showed up after the shooting of Ketchum. Right then he just didn't care what happened next, but somehow, something had clicked over inside him when he had recognized Lang Hewitt.

And realized just how far down the ladder the man had fallen; he hadn't only missed his step, he had dropped like a stone. And landed in a whiskey-barrel by the smell of his breath.

Nevada realized that he could end up the same way, on the long downhill fall to oblivion, and he knew in a flash of bright understanding that Ellie would not approve. She would understand his need to go after the men who had killed her and ruined his life, but she would expect him to put that behind him now, make a new life.

Not that he really felt like doing it, but – *Oh, Ellie! I miss you so much and now that I've finally tracked down all your murderers I-I just dunno what to do. But I know you well enough that you wouldn't want me to just pine away and wither – yet I ain't got any enthusiasm for anything . . . but seeing a man like Hewitt was come down to this – well, it don't attract me an' that in itself tells me I ain't about to let it happen. . . .*

Hewitt stopped at Nevada's query. 'What happens now? To you – or me?'

'You're in the saddle.'

Hewitt snorted. 'Not so spry now, eh? Realized you're on the wrong side of the bars. Well, Nevada Hawk, you just set there and wait my pleasure. I know what to do. I have to investgate this. Oh, and I will. You got my word on that.' Hewitt gave him a tight, crooked, mirthless grin. 'I just dunno how long it's gonna take me!'

Two days later, Amelia Corey came to visit him in the cell. She was wearing her widow's weeds and he couldn't see her face properly behind the lowered veil. She smelled of lavender but her voice was cold and totally unforgiving.

'I just want you to know that I'll do everything in my power to see you dangling at the end of a rope,' she said. 'This is the third time I've been widowed and the first when my husband has been murdered in cold blood. Don't expect to get away with it, Nevada Hawk, or whatever you call yourself! You'll find that I'm just as unforgiving and relentless as you in meting out my own brand of justice when I have been wronged.'

'I'm sorry you got caught up in this, ma'am,' Nevada said, coming to the bars, meaning the words. 'But if you knew the full story. . . .'

'I intend to know it – and however it turns out, I will still hold you responsible for my present widowhood – and you will pay for it! I can be a patient woman when I really and truly want something, Nevada Hawk! And – I – want – you – dead!'

She struck at him through the bars with the black umbrella she carried and he wasn't quite fast enough to get out of range. The brass ferrule on the bottom caught him above the eye, splitting the flesh, making the blood flow.

He heard her give a little sigh of satisfaction as he clapped a hand swiftly over the wound, and then she was hurrying away down the passage, her heels clip-clopping on the flagstones.

'You'll be hearing from me – murderer!'

Holding a kerchief over the bleeding cut, he shook his head slowly and went back to sit on the edge of the bunk.

He had to get out of here. He couldn't stay in this town. He was just about broke but riding the grubline was no new thing for him. Hewitt's comedown was still irritating him; he knew it was stupid, but he felt the longer he stayed near the man, the more chance he had of ending up like him.

Didn't make any logic, but that was the feeling he had. He was also astute enough to realize it was a reaction to all he had done this last year. The bitter hatred and driving need for revenge had kept him going, overridden his grief and everything else. Now it was at an end.

And he had the uncomfortable feeling that there was no place to go, unless he made a place. And he couldn't do that from behind bars.

He hadn't seen Hewitt in days. A half-Mex girl from one of the cantinas brought him food night and morning, told him the sheriff had arranged it. But she didn't know where he was. He had ridden out of town two days ago and hadn't said when he would be back. Or where he was going.

Nevada silently cursed the man. *Just as likely to have*

thrown a drunk somewhere and was sleeping it off – might not even remember he had a prisoner waiting back in the cells when he eventually came round. . . .

One thing – Widow Ketchum hadn't visited him again. He was thankful for that. He hated to admit it, but she kind of bothered him. He made a point of asking the Mex girl about it when she brought him his supper that night.

'Mrs Corey, you mean ? No, I haven't seen her. She does not come to my part of town, señor.'

He could believe that. As she was leaving, she turned and said slowly: 'I think maybe she take the stage to Santa Fe. There is not anything here for her kind now that she has no big *casa* on the hill, where she can look down on the rest of us.'

Nevada smiled thinly; it sounded just like his impression of Amelia Ketchum, too. The only other person he saw was a nameless temporary deputy who never spoke a word when he came to let Nevada out long enough to empty the slop-bucket. Otherwise, his lonely sojourn gave him plenty of time to think. Maybe too much time. . . .

Hewitt turned up the very next day, trail-grimed and unshaven. He had obviously been sleeping in his clothes and he stank of sweat and horses and camp-fire smoke. Nevada stepped back a couple paces when he caught a whiff of the man's sour breath through the bars. He smelt of whiskey, too.

'You are one big pain in the ass, Nevada,' was Hewitt's greeting, the man scrubbing a hand around his jowls.

'Seem to've heard that before. Thanks for arranging my meals, Hewitt, but I'd rather move out and cook my own grub – somewhere a long way from Castle Rock.'

Lang Hewitt leaned his shoulders against the passage wall and fought to make a cigarette with shaky fingers. He mangled it badly and stared at the mess of spilled tobacco and torn paper, bleary-eyed. Nevada realized the man was still drunk, shook his head, took out his tobacco sack and built a cigarette for the lawman. Hewitt stared at it when Nevada handed it to him through the bars.

The sheriff scowled but got the smoke between his lips, leaned his head towards the flame of the vesta Nevada struck on the cell wall. He murmured something that might have been 'thanks', drew deeply, exhaled, and squinted at the prisoner. 'Found out a little about you, mister. Seems you're pretty well known along the cattle trails. And your story about what happened to your wife checks out. Even down to the gang that done it. Led by someone named Linus Ketchum.'

'You knew him as Jim Corey, your land agent.'

Hewitt nodded, swayed slightly, seemed to be thinking hard about his next words. 'Seems to match the description pretty good. Man had power in this town. *Money* power, thanks to Amelia. Her other two husbands left her well off. Think she really fell for Corey – Ketchum. Ploughed most of her money into his business and that big damn house.' He laughed suddenly, shook his head, but didn't let Nevada in on the joke, whatever it was. 'Yeah. He was powerful but he weren't respected. Fact, Corey ruined a lotta folk around here with his snide land deals, cheated 'em. Tried to lease the land then to the mining companies over the mesa. . . .' He drew on the cigarette which was becoming limp from too much saliva now. He stared at it owlishly, glanced up and gave a start when he saw Nevada at the bars. 'Damn if I know what to do about you. You killed four men and it checks out as self-defence every time – tho' could mebbe make things hard for you, the way you prodded Corey, Ketchum, or whoever, into goin' for his gun. You needled him into it.'

'He reached first – you've got half the town who'll bear witness to that.'

Hewitt nodded, kept nodding, and reached out for the wall to steady himself. He dropped the mangled cigarette and idly stepped on it. 'I'm gonna turn you loose, Nevada.'

The prisoner's hands tightened around the bars, not believing his ears; he hadn't really been expecting this but was damned if he was going to look a gift horse in the mouth. 'I'm ready, anytime, Sheriff.'

'Uh-huh. Get the key in a minute. Tell you why. You stay put and – well, hell, what'm I gonna do with you? Widow Amelia's quit town – seen her and she says she's feelin' poorly again, goin' to some sawbones she's heard about . . . hasn't left no charges agin you for burnin' down her house. Half the town, like you said, seen you square off with Corey – Ket – you know who I mean. The other three tried to kill you in your room. . . .' The lawman spread his arms, staggered a little. 'What's there to do? You ain't

wanted for nothin' else I can find out about. . . .
Nope. Might's well let you go, get you outta my hair
– but. . . .' He paused, shook a finger at the cell door.
'But you're trouble, mister, so you don't stick around
my town, you savvy. . . ?'

Nevada nodded and Hewitt shouted: '*Say so,
damnit!*'

'Yeah, I savvy. And I say *muchas gracias*, too. . . . You
want to get those keys now?'

Hewitt shrugged, started away down the passage,
paused and looked back over his shoulder.

'One time – not so long ago – I'd find somethin'
to hang on you – mebbe hang *you*! But now – hell, I
dunno. Just don't seem to have the time or energy –
interest – or somethin' . . .'

'You're doing fine, Hewitt. Just fine,' Nevada said
hoping the man wouldn't pass out in his office
before he brought the keys and opened the cell
door. 'You're doing real good, Sheriff.'

Hell, here he was shouting lies to the town drunk
just because he wanted something from him. . . .

Christ! What did that say about him.

Asa Poole had the chestnut saddled and ready, the
buckskin with a lead rope already attached to the
bridle.

'You owe me for the extra days,' the hostler said.

'Have to put it on my tab, Poole. I'm bust.'

'Ah, I wasn't gonna take any more money from
you. You done a lotta folk a favour gunnin' down that
Lew Abbott and the two deadbeats he hired to blast
you.' Poole suddenly winked. 'An' I don't reckon Jim

38

Corey'll be missed much. As for Amelia, was only her money made folk tip their hats to her.'

He thrust out a big, gnarled hand and, a trifle surprised, Nevada gripped briefly with him.

'There's some grub in a sack on the cantle – see you through a couple of days on the trail if you go careful.'

Nevada swung up into the saddle, settled, looped the lead rope around the horn. 'Obliged, Poole.'

'Too bad you don't pin on Hewitt's badge. He's harmless but he don't do the town much good as a lawman.'

'Not my line. *Adios.*'

Nevada rode slowly through the double doorway and down Main, heading back towards the mesa trail, the way he had first come into town.

He still felt kind of strange. For a year, whenever he had left a town it was because he had a new trail to follow, one that would, he hoped, take him closer to Ketchum and his gang. One by one he had found them, killed them. Now – well, there was a new trail awaiting him, all right, but first he had to find it. Then. . . ?

Where would it lead?

As he started up to the mesa, he realized that, once more, he didn't really care.

CHAPTER 4

FROM AMELIA
WITH LOVE

There were ranches over the mesa as well as the big
mine companies eroding the countryside in their
search for silver, gold, or any other rich mineral that
would bring in dollars by the wagonload. Copper was
the main one being worked at this time, with some
zinc and a little iron.

He paused on a ledge, rolled a cigarette and, while
he smoked it, gazed out over the land for as far as he
could see before the heat haze screened it off or
distorted everything. There was a river and several
creeks that ran into it, smoke came from a tall stack
rising from amongst scattered low timber buildings.
The mines. Closer, there were pastures and a couple
of unmistakable ranch houses but he could not judge
the size of the spreads from here. They looked pretty
big to him, though, and he saw a number of riders,

some single horsemen, others in tight working groups. And he caught a glimpse of one man on the slopes who appeared to have pack-horses trailing him.

Cattle dotted the slopes and browsed along the creekbanks. Two smaller cabins might have been line camps, less than a mile apart but on different spreads if the blur of a barbed-wire fence between meant anything.

Well, he might as well try his luck down there for a job, even a temporary one. At least it would put some decent grub in his belly and a few dollars in his pocket. He just hoped that the valley down there would be far enough away from Castle Rock so he wouldn't be bothered by Lang Hewitt. 'Bothered' was the right word, for the man did bother him, was hanging there at the edge of his thoughts.

And he had no idea why, apart from a sneaking feeling that he felt sorry for the sheriff. He had seen him once in Tombstone, facing down a lynch mob with tough talk and a single-barrelled shotgun; it later turned out he had only the one shell for it. He didn't threaten, simply told them they were in the wrong, that it was his job to protect the man in his jail whom they wanted to lynch, and that was what he aimed to do. He had taken oath-of-office and that was his authority. That, and his guns.

'Rest is up to you fellers.'

Three men had decided they wanted to string up Hewitt's prisoner no matter what. They tried to rush him from three sides; he killed the first man with the shotgun, dropped it, and before it hit the ground,

41

had his sixgun out, shooting the legs from under the other two. The rest of the mob backed up smartly.

Hewitt had picked up the empty shotgun, raked them with a hard stare, then holstered his smoking revolver. 'Go on home, men. Go tell your womenfolk what a son of a bitch the new sheriff is, but make sure they know that when I say somethin', I don't do it just to hear the sound of my own sweet voice.'

It was the coolest thing Nevada had ever seen, and he found it hard to equate that Tombstone lawman with the sorry drunk now mouldering away in a dump like Castle Rock.

Damnit! He had to quit thinking about Hewitt. Whatever the man had become, he had made himself that way and there was nothing Nevada could do about it.

Or even wanted to.

Irritably, he crushed out the unfinished cigarette against the saddlehorn, tossed the extinguished butt on to a flat rock and heeled the chestnut forward and down.

The trail steepened quickly below the ledge and he had to concentrate on working both horses safely around the tight bends. Half-way down, with boulders jutting precariously from the slope above him, a rifle crashed, slamming echoes through the afternoon. A bullet whipped the battered hat from his head.

It spun to the ground and he was a split second behind it, shoulder-rolling into brush, taking his rifle with him. Breath jarred from his body as he kicked a way into and under the brush, which was raked by

42

three more hasty shots. They were close and a spinning rock reopened the small cut on his forehead where Amelia Corey had struck him with her umbrella. He wiped blood out of his eye, crawled deeper into the sparse cover. Twigs fell on his shoulders and the back of his neck. Lead burned across his upper left arm, tearing his shirt, but barely breaking the skin. Another shot lifted his long tangled hair as it passed, wafting a small breeze over his forehead.

It was only a matter of time before one of those shots nailed him dead centre. He was too close to the bushwhacker who had the advantage of high ground. *Only one thing to do – and it was not without risk!*

But staying put held plenty of risk so he abruptly reared up out of the brush and flung himself bodily downhill. It took the killer by surprise and he had to shift aim hurriedly. He got off two quick shots and Nevada gave him credit for that. One whipped air past his face, whined off a rock just below where he was falling. He twisted his body, landed half-turned on his back, kicked his boots against a larger rock and propelled himself behind a weathered deadfall.

Two more bullets chewed splinters from the log and he heard through the blood pounding in his head the click of the man's rifle hammer. *Time for him to reload!*

Which was also time for Nevada to make his move, gamble on getting up the slope and into a position where he could see the rifleman before he was stopped in his tracks.

No use thinking about all the risks: get it done!

He thrust up and got his legs working fast, veering

around the deadfall, hitting the upslope below his orginal position, seeing that his mounts had had enough sense to find shelter amongst some boulders. Breath barking, sweat flying, legs pounding, he strained and crashed his way through the line of half-dead brush. He glimpsed a red-checked shirt and a brown hat as the man up there saw him and frantically tried to complete his reloading.

Fool! He should have worked the lever, got a shell into the breech from those already in the magazine and picked off Nevada in mid-stride. Instead, he kept trying to stuff shells into the tube, fumbling and dropping two.

He never had a chance to drop any more.

Nevada suddenly propped, digging in with his boots, tensing his body muscles to halt his forward motion as if he had hit an invisible wall. The rifle butt pressed into his hip and he worked lever and trigger in three prolonged, thundering, shots, the sound hammering across the mesa.

There were no ricochets, because all three drove into the killer and he was flung back violently, arms flapping wide, rifle clattering as he went over backwards and hung there. His eyes were staring, his blood glinting in the sunlight.

Standing over him, Nevada didn't recognize him, but hunkered down as he saw there was a little life left in the man. 'I dunno you.'

The glazing eyes held to his sweaty, dirt-grimed face.

'Someone pay you to bushwhack me?' No response and before Nevada could frame a third question, the man's eyes closed, he coughed up a gurgling throatful of blood and slumped.

Searching the body, Nevada found an old envelope with the name of P. MacDaniel, care of general delivery, Castle Rock, New Mexico Territory in blurred and faded ink. Then in another pocket he found a bank receipt for fifty dollars, deposited in McDaniel's name.

'Is that all I'm worth?' he murmured with a crooked smile, sniffing the bloodstained envelope.

Despite the gunsmoke in his nostrils he still smelled lavender quite plainly.

No wonder Amelia hadn't bothered to have him charged with arson.

It turned out to be one of those days: things started out OK with his release by Hewitt, went bad when that bushwhacker had used him for target practice, and now, in his night camp, things again seemed to be headed for hell in a hand-basket.

Once down from the mesa, cutting across range with wide patches of lush grass dotted with cowpats, he figured to make an early camp. There were leaden clouds forming over the range at the far end of the valley and a sniff of ozone in the air that presaged a storm.

He found a place under a jutting ledge of rock that ought to keep him tolerably dry from the slope's run-off when the rain started. There were black smudges on the underside of the rock and some burnt-down twigs on the floor. Seemed this had been used as a camping-place before.

He built a small fire, enough to cook the strips of venison Asa Poole had put in his grubsack. They might have been a bit past its best but he ate them fast enough, drank some coffee that was too weak but welcome. He rolled his after-supper smoke as the first drops of rain started to fall and lightning snagged across the sky. There was a lot more lightning and claps of thunder but the rain wasn't all that heavy. Heavy enough, though, to mask the approach of a trio of riders who suddenly appeared on the downslope below his camp. He stood quickly, dropping his half-finished cigarette into the dying fire. The next streak of lightning glinted off ponchos and hard-planed faces staring down at him.

'Who the hell're you?' demanded the rugged-looking man in the middle, leaning big hands on his saddle horn.

'Who's asking?'

'You'll find out – after you tell me your name.'

Nevada held the raw gaze from those pale-blue eyes, saw the recklessness there, the urge to make trouble. Warily, he said: 'They call me Nevada.'

It didn't do anything for the tough-looking ranny, but a slim rider on his left leaned to the side and said a shade tightly: 'He's the one killed Corey and Lew Abbott, as well as them hardcases at the Creekside, Bo.'

The big man looked at Nevada more closely now. 'That right?'

'Hewitt's satisfied it was self-defence.'

Bo laughed briefly. 'Don't go wettin' yourself! We got no beef over that scum takin' up residence in

Boot Hill.' Then his voice hardened. 'But we got a beef with you makin' camp on Broken T range.'

Nevada hitched an eyebrow. 'That where I am? I just came over the mesa and camped when I saw the storm brewing.'

Their sudden tension showed even under their drooping ponchos as the rain rattled against the stiff, gleaming material. 'That you doin' the shootin' we heard up there earlier?' the one called Bo asked curtly, nodding towards the unseen mesa.

Nevada hesitated, then, looking at them squarely, nodded. 'Killed a snake.'

'Wasted a lot of lead by the sound of it.'

'Got him in the end. Think his name was McDaniel.'

'Judas, Bo!' gasped the rider on his right. 'Phil McDaniel! He'd hire his gun to the devil hisself!'

Nevada swore under his breath. 'I hope he weren't a pard of yours, because he tried to bushwhack me.' He showed them the torn sleeve and bullet burn on his arm. They didn't look impressed, but they dismounted now and crowded under the ledge as the rain increased.

'You just attract trouble, don't you, mister? Like maggots to a carcass.'

'I got a notion Mrs Ketchum – Corey – figured she should square with me for killing her husband.' Nevada didn't explain although they waited as if expecting him to.

'Last I heard, Bo,' said the slim rider, 'McDaniel was workin' for Corey, ridin' roughshod over them sodbusters he wanted off the riverbottom land.'

Bo nodded slowly.'Who you workin' for?'

'No one. Figured I might try one of the spreads.'

Bo snorted. 'You better not try Broken T!'

'I'll take whatever work I can get. I'm broke.'

Bo shook his head. 'Just clear this valley, mister. We don't need your kind here.'

'I'll ride on through – after I earn a few bucks to put in my pocket.'

Bo stiffened and the other two glanced at him. The slim one moved to the fire and kicked the embers. He spoke to the other rider. 'Toss some kindlin' on, Mike. I can do with some coffee.'

Nevada was a shade slow; he kept his attention on Bo, figuring that was where the trouble would come from. But the other two suddenly ran in, one from either side, and Mike, who had picked up some kindling, swiped at him with the dead branch. Nevada threw up an arm, took the blow, and the deadwood broke. By then Slim had his arms around him and was trying to pin him. He bucked and struggled but his boots slipped and he went down to one knee.

Bo was waiting, his poncho was pushed back now and he tugged his work-gloves tighter as he took a step forward and drove a punch into Nevada's midriff. The drifter grunted and doubled as far as the others would let him. Bo had his boots planted now; he drove three more jarring blows into his body and smashed another into his face.

Nevada let his legs sag – it was really no effort! – and they eased their grips to let him fall. Instead, he lunged at Bo, got a grip on the man's damp shirt-front and drove the top of his head into the man's face. Bo yelled and floundered back, eventually going down to one knee, head hanging, beads of bright blood dripping from his nostrils and mouth, spotting the wet ground. Nevada avoided the clawing hands of the cowboys and kicked Bo in the chest, stretching him out.

Slim and the other man moved in, Mike swinging his branch again. Nevada took the blow on the shoulder and he spun, slipped, and put a hand down. Slim stepped in, kicking. Nevada took one blow, grabbed the boot the second time and dragged the man in front of Mike and his piece of deadwood.

Slim yelled as he tried to dodge, felt the impact on his head, and fell, floundering in mud. The other man stopped, startled. Nevada came upright, took the branch from the man's hand and slammed him across the side of the head. He fell hard beside Slim. Nevada spun as he heard the rustle of a poncho behind him.

Bo was pushing the stiff folds aside, reaching for his gun. But he froze when he found himself looking at the gleaming Colt covering him, held rock-steady in Nevada's hand.

'Leave it, Bo!'

Bo Whelan slowly lifted his hands, looking mighty warily at Nevada now, sniffing and spitting blood. 'You're hell on wheels, ain't you?'

Nevada ignored him, took a couple of steps back so he could watch the other two as well. They were both looking mighty sick and sorry right now, staring apprehensively at Nevada.

'You always ride strangers like this?'

'If they camp on Broken T without my say-so,' growled Bo, unrepentant. 'I need to get my kerchief out!'

Nevada nodded and watched carefully as Bo worked a grubby kerchief out of a pants pocket and held it to his bloody face, murderous eyes glittering at Nevada above the crumpled cloth.

Slim glared at the other ranny. 'You damn fool! You near brained me!'

'Take more'n hunk of deadwood to bust that hard head of yours,' growled Mike.

'Hell with you, you son of a bitch!'

'Stay put,' Nevada said as the men moved towards each other. They stopped, stared at him – and at the gun in his hand.

'You handle that Colt pretty damn good,' Bo Whelan opined, squinting a little. 'You wouldn't be workin' for Harding, would you? Heard he was bringin' in gunfighters. He tryin' to plant you on us to make it easier for him to grab our land?'

'Dunno Harding from a lump of cheese. I been in Castle Rock since I arrived. Hewitt turned me loose after noon and McDaniel kind of delayed me some. This looked like the best place to shelter from the rain. And that's as much as I'm explaining.' He jerked the gun. 'Shuck your hardware – carefully! And your ponchos. Then start walking.'

'In this!'

Nevada merely looked back coldly. 'I'll turn your horses loose come daylight. But if I see you anywhere near my camp, or hear a sound, I'll be shooting first and asking questions afterwards. Now move!'

When they started down the muddy slope, becoming soaked in seconds now that the rain was pounding down harder, Bo Whelan turned once to look back, his hat dripping, blood still oozing from his nostrils and split lips.

'We ever meet again, gun or no gun, I'm gonna tear your goddamn head off!'

'OK,' Nevada said easily, then suddenly fired two shots into the mud at Bo's feet. Bo danced involuntarily, cursing. Slim and Mike started to run down the slope. Whelan turned and began jog-trotting, too.

In minutes they had disappeared into the rain-lashed darkness and Nevada turned and kicked dirt over the fire.

No sense in making an easy target, even for men he believed were unarmed.

Not in this damn dangerous neck of the woods.

CHAPTER 5

BUY ANY
MAN'S GUN

Barbara Tate looked at the three muddy, dishevelled men who stood on the porch of her ranch house without sympathy. She was a tall woman, favoured trousers-and-shirt working-outfits to crinoline or gingham feminine attire. She was wearing clean but crumpled corduroy trousers now and a blue-and-grey checkered shirt with the sleeves rolled up above the elbows. She pushed some of her thick straw-coloured hair back from her face.

'Well, look at you. Horses run off?'

Rain was still falling, but the storm was passing over now, sheet-lightning only flickering beyond the hills.

'Taken from us by some damn gunfighter!' Slim White growled. 'Up at Tomcat Ridge. He—'

'Shut up!' snapped Bo Whelan and for the first

time she saw his busted mouth and the smeared blood in the lamplight. 'Go get cleaned up. You, too, Mike!'

Barbara said nothing as they slouched away, muttering. She waited and when Bo turned back towards her, said: 'He got the better of you, too, did he, Bo?'

He flushed but it wasn't obvious in the dim light and with all the mud and rain and blood on his rugged face.

Smiling a little, she asked: 'Who was he?'

'Nevada, he calls himself. The one who killed Jim Corey and Lew Abbot in town accordin' to Slim.'

'Well, he was there and saw it so he'd know.' Barbara's oval face was sober now. 'You'd better come in and have a drink – just leave those boots at the door.'

On his second whiskey, standing in his sodden, holey socks on a straw mat in the living-room, Whelan told the woman his story.

'Why'd you ride him so hard?'

He shrugged. 'Just lettin' him know he couldn't camp where he liked – not on Broken T land.'

'Spoiling for a fight is another way of putting it, Bo. You've got too big a chip on your shoulder.'

'I ain't heard many complaints from you.'

Her green eyes flickered. 'Watch your mouth! You're still just another hired hand, Bo. You tend to forget that.'

'I was more'n that to your father, and your brother, when he was runnin' things!'

'Ty and Dad're both long dead and I'm running

things my way now. Ty was too soft. That's how we lost so much land when the mines moved in. He didn't fight hard enough, soon enough. But I'll fight as long as I have breath in my body! And picking fights with drifters is not part of my plan. And it better not be part of yours from now on.'

He had heard it all before; it was water off a duck's back.

'Well, I figure this Nevada might've been sent for by Harding.'

'The way I heard it, he had a score to settle with Jim Corey.'

'Claims Corey's real name was Ketchum, was some kinda outlaw. But this Nevada's tough – and fast!' Bo shook his head slowly. 'Never seen a gun come out so quick.'

Barbara showed interest now. 'Do you think he works for Harding, then?'

'Either that or he's on his way to see him. A gunslinger good as he is ain't outta work for long.'

'Mmmm, no.' She poured another drink, motioned impatiently for Bo to do the same. 'Sounds like the kind of man we need to stand up to Harding . . . not let him go work for him.'

Bo paused with the bottle-neck against his glass, snapping up his head.

'Well?' she asked curtly. 'Doesn't he?'

Bo filled his glass and sipped before answering. 'Mebbe,' he said reluctantly.

'Oh, you don't like him because he bested you, Bo, but set that aside. *Isn't* he the kind of man we need to fight Harding?'

'Hell, me and the boys're doin' all right!'

'Not that I've noticed. The mine's run-off is still fouling Banjo Creek and there's no compensation forthcoming for the cattle that've been poisoned.'

'Well, we kicked off Harding's hardcases, din' we?'

She sighed. 'But that's not the level of resistance we need to show! We need to be defensive, yet tough enough to drive him right out of the county, or close the mine down. I know it's no easy job, and we have to tread carefully, but it can be done, even if the other spreads are slow to get involved. But what we need is someone to show Harding he can't ride over us roughshod. Not without paying dearly for it.'

Bo pursed his lips, winced at the sting and shook his head dubiously. 'Ty would never've gone for that. Your Dad might've but Barbara, you start a real range war and we're gonna have the law down on our necks like a landslide. The mine'll be the one smellin' of roses!'

'You're afraid of someone like Lang Hewitt?' she asked, her contempt clear.

He straightened involuntarily. 'Hell, no one but a kid'd be scared of that drunk Hewitt! But he could easily send for a federal marshal, and he likely would. He don't have enough nerve to do anythin' about it himself.'

'So, if we have to fight, it's best to get it over and done with before Hewitt does send for a marshal.'

Bo frowned, fingers whitening as they tightened around his shotglass. 'You ain't gonna offer this Nevada a job?'

'I'm thinking about it. Bo, Dad opened up this

place, he fought Indians and thieves to make it the way it is – *was!* We've lost all the land I intend to lose to the mining companies. You know how Jim Corey took that south-west corner because Dad had forgotten to file on it, too. So maybe Nevada did us a favour by killing Corey. So – I owe him something for that.'

Bo Whelan was dead against it, that was clear. He tossed down his drink, picked up his hat and made towards the door, his wet socks squelching quietly.

'Well, you'll do what you want, I guess, Barbara. Like always!'

'And it's my intention that I always will! Get some sleep, Bo. You look like you need it.'

Scowling, he went out into the darkness.

What he needed was another crack at this Nevada! And by God, he'd have it – one way or another! And he didn't aim to ask any damn female's permission, either!

When Nevada walked his chestnut around the bend, he reined down fast, dropping the spare mount's lead-rope and slapping a hand to his gun butt. The rider sitting squarely in the middle of the track lifted a staying hand languidly. 'Don't get nervous, friend. I was looking for a man with two pack-horses, been wandering across our land and I'd like a word with him. Seen him? No. . . ? Well, you might be the one they call Nevada. Do I suppose correctly?'

Apart from having a dislike for fancy speech, Nevada was leery of the rider. He looked to be average size, but his clothes were too neat for Nevada's liking. He sported a dark-brown hat, carefully

56

creased dead centre through the crown, barbered brown hair, was clean-shaven except for a thin pencil moustache drawing a line above his upper lip – and the lip was thin, the mouth like a slash in the narrow, bony face. The eyes were restless, taking in every inch of Nevada so that he felt that the man could count the change in his pockets.

The shirt was narrow-weave corduroy, chocolate-brown, the trousers of similar material, only lighter. He wore only one gun which didn't look any different from a hundred other Peacemakers Nevada had seen – except it was gleaming, the blued metal deeply polished. The long-fingered hands were encased in soft chamois gloves, also dark brown.

'Suppose away. Who're you?'

Teeth flashed briefly, white and even. 'Calvin Judd. Personal assistant to Mr Kyle Harding of the Amarosa Mining Company.' He jerked his head slightly over his left shoulder but Nevada didn't bother shifting his gaze as he was supposed to. He had seen the high, smoking chimneystacks when topping out on the ridge behind him.

A slight frown creased Judd's forehead but only very briefly. He gave a small nod, as if confirming something to himself. 'You know how powerful the mines are in this part of the territory, I take it?'

Nevada shook his head. 'Dunno and don't care. Unless they're offering jobs.'

'Ah! Now that is convenient, my friend, because I was working around to asking if you might be looking for work.'

'Just one thing, Judd. I ain't your friend. Dunno

57

you from Redeye Billy, the town drunk back in Tombstone.'

Judd's eyes narrowed and they were strangely like flint now. 'Well. There is some gain in being outspoken, I suppose, although it does give good manners something of the old heave-ho. But I suspect you're being deliberately rude.'

'I can be good-mannered when there's a need.'

They locked gazes for long seconds, then Calvin Judd nodded slightly. 'Fair enough. I suppose, if you're the jumpy sort I did startle you, appearing in front of you like that.'

'Almost enough for me to've put a bullet through your head.'

Judd smiled, chuckled, shook his head slightly.

'Well, no, I don't believe so, my fr – Nevada! There is just the possibility that I could be fast enough to get off the first shot – under any circumstances you care to name.'

'Well, unless you want to die right now, I guess we might's well leave this conversation.' Nevada spoke easily and Judd realized that the man hadn't dropped his hand from the cedar butt of his sixgun all this time. As his cocky smile faded, Nevada put his hand back on his thigh and Judd's sharp gaze saw the notches. His lips moved faintly as he counted.

'Five dead men, I see. How long did it take you to get that tally?'

'Just over a year.'

'A year! Fr – Man, if I started notching my guns for every man I've killed, why, I wouldn't have any butts left! Just the skeletal frames!'

'I don't make a habit of it. Just wanted to keep firm tally. Well, Judd. Why're you still blocking my trail?'

Judd grinned. 'You're telling me I'd best move or you'll make me?' Nevada said nothing and at last Judd shrugged. 'Mr Harding would like to see you. There's a possibility you just might be offered work. Providing you meet certain . . . requirements.'

'What kind of work?'

'Can you afford to be choosy, Nevada?'

Nevada sighed. 'Not right now,' he admitted. 'All right – seems some folk in the valley believe I'm already Harding's man, so what the hell?'

'I'll tell you. There's one hell of a difference between being thought to be working for Amarosa and actually doing it. Who was it thought you worked for Mr Harding? And what did you do that would make them consider such thoughts?'

Nevada told him briefly of his meeting with Bo Whelan and the two Broken T men. Judd listened silently, then burst out laughing. He slapped a gloved hand on to his thigh.

'I would've dearly loved to have witnessed that! When Mr Harding hears that story, I believe he'll hire you on the spot! Barbara Tate will be mad as a hornet that she hasn't already put her brand on you.'

That wasn't the way Nevada would have put it but he said nothing, allowed Judd to set his fine buckskin with a black blaze between its eyes alongside. They headed away from the direction Nevada had been taking and started climbing towards the mines and the buildings scattered across the slope where the creek tumbled in a green-and-white frothing waterfall.

*

Kyle Harding's face was an almost perfect oval, his hair smoothed to his head by some brilliantine or pomade that had a subtle fragrance Nevada couldn't put a name to. Some kind of spice, he thought. The miner was about fifty, slim and fit-looking, not hand-some, but not ugly, either. His frock-coat and suit were impeccable, made of some expensive cloth, cut to almost hide the shoulder holster Harding favoured – but not quite. The furniture in the large office was solid oak and teak and – well, everything reeked of high quality which meant high expense.

Harding had conferred with Judd in private briefly, leaving Nevada in a waiting-room after furnishing the drifter with a cigar that must have cost at least a silver dollar-and-a-half. When Judd appeared in the office doorway and jerked his head, Nevada went in, enjoying the elegant smoke.

'Never had a cigar that tasted as good as this, Mr Harding,' he allowed as he stood on the deep-pile carpet in front of the desk.

Harding allowed himself a thin smile. 'Trying to put me in the right mood, Nevada?'

Nevada shrugged and the other two could see that it was no affectation; the man really didn't give much of a damn whether he was hired or not. He was will-ing to be polite but if Harding told him to light a shuck he would do it just as easily and readily as if the man offered him a high-paying job.

Which is what Harding did.

'On Calvin's recommendation – and with what I

60

have seen of you with my own eyes and assessed – I have decided to offer you a job with the company, Nevada. You'll be paid fifty dollars a week and will be answerable only to Mr Judd or myself. Accept or reject?'

'Gimme a minute to catch my breath! Fifty a *week*! Man, I never even earned fifty a month when I was trail boss.'

'Mr Harding pays well and expects the best service and total loyalty in return,' Judd said kind of smugly, but hard-eyed. '*Total* loyalty, Nevada.'

'Heard you the first time.' Nevada looked from one man to another. 'What do I have to do?'

Judd bristled. 'What do you care? You've just told us that fifty dollars a week is more money than you've ever made before—'

'I didn't say that. I said it was more than I earned in a month as trail boss. At one time I averaged a couple of thousand a week, sometimes more.'

The others frowned, looked at each other. Judd said slowly: 'That could be misconstrued as an admission that you once rode a . . . lawless trail?'

'That what it sounded like? Nah – I'm talking about a time I was hunting buffalo in Texas, on the Staked Plains. During the big migration we killed a thousand a week, and it was just when buffalo robes were all the rage back East. We were lucky, came in right at the beginning, went clear through to the end, then, when it fell off, we traded to the Indians for gold nuggets and I bought a ranch. Years ago now, but I'm expecting this job'll mean less hard work than running buffalo.'

Harding chuckled. 'Calvin, you have a devious, suspicious mind!'

Judd scowled. 'I think I walked into that one.'

Nevada's deadpan face gave nothing away – but there could have been a slight twinkle in his eyes. 'What did you have in mind for me to do, Mr Harding?'

'Mr Judd'll tell you – outside.' That was Harding's way of dismissing them and in Judd's own small office – not much more than a cubicle – the man said briefly:

'The ranchers are giving us a hard time of it because our run-off from the extraction plant is fouling their creeks. Amarosa has built sluices and carry-off drains, elevated so the spill is dumped beyond the creeks, but the ranches claim it soaks back through the soil and contaminates the water anyway, and is killing their cattle.'

'Well, that's a real possibility. I've seen it happen before. Not with mines as big as Amarosa, but smaller outfits can foul drinking-water just as easily. There a range war?'

'Not yet. Not full-blown, but it's heading that way. This Barbara Tate is kind of an unofficial leader of the ranchers and she's a fighter. Bo Whelan is her troubleshooter and he's tough. You might care to watch your back when you're riding for us.'

Nevada pursed his lips. 'Well, now – I've hired out my gun before, but I think I'll mebbe take another look around the valley before I sign on.'

Judd stiffened. 'You've already accepted!'

'Not really. All I did was ask Harding what he

wanted me to do; now you've told me and I don't care for it much.' He held up a hand as Judd, face hard and flushed now, started to speak. 'I'm a cattleman at heart, Judd. I've seen cows poisoned before, loco weed, some vindictive son of a bitch throwing a dead coyote into the only water for a hundred miles, another tossing in a can full of strychnine – and I've seen cows die from polluted water from mineral runoff. Copper sulphate, cyanide wash, sulphur dioxide. It ain't pretty and if that's what's happening here, I'd tend to lean towards the ranchers rather than fight 'em.'

Judd's eyes were no more than slits now. And suddenly his Peacemaker was in his hand. Nevada hitched up both eyebrows; it had taken him by surprise. He had never seen a man draw so fast.

'I can see you ain't a man who makes idle boasts, Judd. But why you putting that gun on me?'

Calvin Judd drew his thin lips tightly across his white teeth and leaned forward slightly. 'Because, *my friend*, if, in your own vernacular, you "ain't with us", then you're "agin us"! Now go out that door and down the side stairs – very carefully! You and I have to reach an understanding. And if you're smart, you'll see things our way.'

Nevada pursed his lips as he moved slowly towards the narrow door to one side of Judd's desk.

'I've never claimed to be particularly smart,' he said quietly.

'Too bad, Nevada! Because you could very well end up dead! Now, *move!*'

CHAPTER 6

HIRED GUN

There was a stairway, narrow and steep, running down the outside wall of the mine building. Harding's and Judd's offices were on the second floor, away from some of the noise of the stamp-mills and crushers, also the fumes from the mineral-washing plants and furnaces to drive the steam-engines.

Nevada stepped out on to the small landing, started down, left hand steadying himself on the rickety rail. Calvin Judd closed the door leading from his office and when he turned to go after Nevada his heart almost stopped.

Nevada had reversed direction, had stepped silently and swiftly up the few steps he had taken down and was now within an arm's length of Judd. The gunfighter brought his Peacemaker around in a blur of speed, twisting, but Nevada's hand reached out and clamped over the cylinder, which was just starting to revolve as Judd instinctively squeezed the trigger. Nevada's grip on the cylinder prevented the gun from firing.

Their gazes locked, both men's eyes hard and ready for anything. Judd curled a lip under his moustache and that signal warned Nevada to expect the man's next move. It was a simple one and could have been mighty effective – except that Nevada Hawk hadn't survived all these years without learning a trick or two.

Judd thrust with his shoulder, hoping to knock Nevada off balance as the man was standing on the very edge of the landing above the first step. Nevada braced himself, at the same time moving to a more sound footing, swinging his weight so that it pulled with Judd's forward movement. Judd grunted and then cursed as the Peacemaker was twisted from his grip as he tried to regain balance. He was dragged forward and all he saw before him was the steep drop-away of the set of stairs. He flailed, looking for some support.

Nevada yanked, stepped aside and heaved hard. Judd yelled loudly as he fell, tumbling and bouncing and somersaulting, crashing his way to the bottom of the stairs where he sprawled on the ground, rolling several feet before coming to a stop. He lay face down, in an awkward heap, unmoving, as Nevada came down swiftly, still holding the man's gun.

There were workmen in that part of the mine and some had seen Judd's fall. Now, watching as Nevada came down the stairs, they sauntered over, rough, tough-looking men in mud-spattered clothes, with big, calloused hands and hard faces.

They stopped a few feet away as Nevada, throwing them a glance, knelt beside Judd. The man had a knot on his forehead over his right eye. There was blood on his face and his clothes were torn and filthy, also spotted with blood. He was out cold but breathing all right. Nevada stood, looking at the men, still holding the Peacemaker.

'That first step's a beaut,' he said, deadpan and the men stared back sullenly.

Then someone chuckled, and another man laughed briefly. Pretty soon most of the tough-looking miners were grinning and someone said: 'Lucky Judd's got a hard head!'

That brought more laughter and Nevada grinned, shucked the shells from the Colt and dropped it beside the unconscious gunman.

'If anyone asks, tell Harding I've changed my mind. I don't want the job.'

'Well, I was you, feller, I wouldn't hang around,' a dark-skinned rangy man said, grim-faced, a mite breathless.

Nevada thought there was Indian blood in him for sure, that high-planed triangular face and the dark eyes were a dead giveaway.

Nevada nodded. As he turned to walk away the dark-skinned man added: 'Take some advice and clear the territory. It won't be good for your health otherwise.'

Nevada paused, but decided the man wasn't making a threat, just giving him what was probably meant as good advice. '*Gracias, amigo.* But can't afford to. Gotta find work somewhere.'

'Stay away from the basin ranches.' This time there was a distinct warning in the dark man's words.

Nevada didn't reply and made his way around the front of the building to where he had left his horses.

Behind him, Calvin Judd began to stir and the dark-skinned man went to kneel beside him and help him to a sitting position. The other miners turned and went back to their jobs. Groggily, Judd growled: 'Help me up, damnit!'

Nevada was working his horses down the last of the steep trail from the mine when he heard a rattle through the leaves on the scraggly trees just above his head, almost instantly followed by the echoing whipcrack of a rifle.

He spurred the chestnut, leaning forward and low in the saddle, hearing another shot as he skidded around a bend, suddenly felt a jarring tension on the lead-rope that almost pulled him from the saddle.

The spare mount whinnied and as Nevada glanced over his shoulder he saw it go down thrashing. He flipped the lead-rope off his saddle and ran the chestnut into thicker timber. Once within the treeline he dismounted, sliding his own Winchester from his scabbard. He heard the buckskin's death throes, then another rifle shot from above and the horse went still. His mouth tightened: *maybe the ambusher was just being humane and putting the horse out of its misery? Maybe.*

But he didn't figure that Calvin Judd had that much humanity in him. It had to be Judd: the man's ego had been damaged by that tumble down the stairs, more greatly than any physical injury he might have sustained. Just to be sure, Nevada, crouching, called:

'How about that face-off now, Judd? You game?'

'Not when I have you pinned, you lousy bastard!'

'What happened to the fancy talk, Judd? Guess that tumble shook you up pretty bad, huh?'

'You'll find out how bad!'

'Nah. Don't think I'll bother to stick around. You don't have the guts to face me fair and square, so I'll be on my way. But we'll meet again, Judd. So keep your Peacemaker oiled.'

Judd didn't reply and Nevada mounted again, worked the chestnut through the timber for a couple of hundred yards before breaking out for the last fast run across open country to the line of trees below, spreading towards the creek.

As he figured, Judd knew this area and had simply moved to a spot where he could cover the open ground. But he hadn't expected Nevada to come out so far along and his first hasty shots were well short. By the time Nevada disappeared into the timber, Judd was just getting the range.

He emptied the rifle in frustrated rage.

Following the creek, still alert for pursuit, riding with his rifle butt on his thigh, Nevada twisted sharply in the saddle, bringing the gun up, as someone called from the shadows.

'What were you shooting at?'

It was a woman's voice and he paused with the rifle across his chest, a shell in the breech, finger on the trigger, hammer cocked. He saw her then, walking a fine-looking line-backed dun out of the clump of trees. She wore a checked shirt with the sleeves rolled back, and work-stained trousers, a battered hat pushed to the back of her head to reveal thick, straw-coloured hair.

'I'm Barbara Tate. You're on Broken T land here.'

'Figured I might be, looking at the creek. I've seen clearer water in a swamper's bucket. This what the mine's run-off is doing to your water supply?'

'That's it.' Barbara was only a few yards from him now. She was openly looking him over but it didn't bother him. He knew she knew who he was and had the feeling that she had actually been out *looking* for him.

He squatted, scooped up a cupped handful of the murky water and sniffed, wrinkling his nose.

'Ain't what you'd call perfume. Doubt that I've come across a cow that'd even think of drinking this.'

She met and held his gaze. 'No – not here. This is too close to the mine, too concentrated. But further downstream, where the creek branches and waters several ranches, it's diluted enough for them to drink. You know how thirsty cattle are. Anything wet will do. Some die, others suffer.'

He nodded. 'Tried fences?'

She gave him a cold look. 'I've been working cattle all my life, mister. I know every way there is to keep cows away from loco weed or bad water or broken country. Of course I've tried fences! I've also tried to catch the men who cut the wire at every opportunity and let my cows through.'

He frowned. 'Then Harding wants you right out of the country, not just to leave his run-off disposal methods be?'

'That's it. Our spreads are apparently built over a whole basin of minerals and Amarosa want them. I don't know them all but there's copper, zinc and someone told me maybe silver – lead, too. Could even be gold for all I know.'

'You could ask a good price then.'

'Which I wouldn't stoop to do! My father, mother, brother and sister are buried on this land. It's Tate land, always has been, and I intend it should stay that way.' She shook her head suddenly, the fair curls spilling partly across her face. 'Amarosa think if they roust us enough we'll sell out dirt-cheap.'

Nevada scrubbed a hand idly around his jaw, hearing the rasp of fresh stubble. 'But you've never asked them to make an offer?'

He saw it was the wrong thing to say, the way her face clouded and she straightened to her full height, every inch of her in high tension. 'Don't you hear well? My father pioneered this land, raised cattle. This land has fed and clothed our family for over twenty years! Why should I abandon my heritage just because some big mining company wants me to?'

'I savvy what you're saying,' Nevada said.

Her features softened. 'Then you'd fight under the same circumstances?'

'Reckon so.' He glanced around, saw cattle dotting slopes a mile or so away. 'Saw some of your herd up close a spell back. They look healthy enough to me. Some of those minerals you mentioned could get into the grass, though, through the roots, make them poorly. Are you sure there's copper and lead here?'

'No-oo. We were just told there could be. But there's nothing wrong with Broken T beef! It's in almost every household in Santa Fe, even as far off as Denver.'

'Which is what I'm getting at. Maybe the "mineral" deposits here – if there are any – are the kind that don't affect the cattle. The water would, sure, if it's contaminated enough, but the ground seems to be clean enough.'

Her frown deepened. 'I'm not sure I understand you.'

'Well, copper, sulphur, lead, even zinc won't do cattle any good if there's too much in their diet. But silver or gold wouldn't harm their feed or their meat at all.'

She stared, then let her shoulders slump as her teeth tugged at her lower lip. 'My – *God*! I never thought to question it! I mean, the mine is processing copper and other raw minerals found in these parts. I thought that's what they were after here. You're saying that they think there's gold or silver in high concentrations on our land? Are trying to kill off our herds by polluting the streams – and drive us all out so they can take over the entire basin! *Cheaply*!'

'Wouldn't be the first time it's happened. Saw it in Arizona, place north of Tucson, in Saguaro country. Chiricahua Apache lived there, peaceful enough, except when they got drunk on their *tulupai* once in

71

a while. But some white prospector, there illegally, found gold and figured there could be a whole reef underfoot. Did a deal with a mining company. They paid him to keep mum, poisoned the water. The Indians were forced to abandon the place and the mining company moved in – poisoned water still washes gold and dilutes cyanide for purifying it. . . .'

She waited, then said: 'It wouldn't've been the Amarosa Mining Company?'

He shook his head. 'No, but mining engineers change jobs almost as much as grubline riders. If something works one place, they'll try it again.'

Barbara nodded gently. 'I take it that you are *persona non grata* at the Amarosa. Does that mean you're open to offers?'

'Depends on the offer.'

'Work for me. I'll pay you fighting wages.'

'Fifty a week?' Her jaw dropped and he smiled crookedly, adding, 'That's what Harding offered, but I knew it was too good to be true. Aw, I reckon he'd've paid it, but it was what I'd have to do to earn it that bothered me.'

Barbara's face was suddenly wary. 'A man of ethics?' He shrugged, looking at her steadily. 'Of course! I believe you took more than a year to track down Jim Corey who you claimed murdered your wife. Yes, I think you are a man who applies himself tenaciously to any chore he's doing. I can only offer you fifty-and-found – that's for a month! But I'll pay you ten dollars bonus for every time you have to use your gun, as long as it's in the defence of Broken T. Private gunfights won't count.'

He sighed. 'Well, I sure ain't gonna make my fortune, am I? But – OK. I've hired out for less. Not much, mind.' Then he grinned. 'How about Bo Whelan?'

She laughed. 'Bo's a hardcase. But I can handle him. You leave him to me. You just worry about Harding and Calvin Judd.'

'I don't aim to worry about 'em, but I'll spare 'em a thought or two, maybe.'

'Let's get back to the ranch house. I don't like being this close to Amarosa land.'

He gestured for her to lead the way and she turned her dun. He followed on the dusty chestnut. 'Who's that?'

She looked where he was pointing to some trees high up. 'I don't see anybody. . . .'

'Gone now. Feller leading a couple of pack-mules. Judd was looking for him earlier.'

'Another drifter, I guess,' she said indifferently. 'The mines hire lots of them. . . . Not all hardcases.'

'And you just let him ride off?' Kyle Harding spoke through his teeth, staring up from under his knitted brows at the battered Judd standing before him.

Calvin Judd was uncomfortable, and not just because he was eating crow, but from the hammering his body had taken during his fall down the steps. And the knowledge that Nevada had ridden off without one of Judd's bullets under his hide.

'He got into that thick stand of timber. By the time I worked around it, he was riding away with Barbara Tate.'

Harding swore, his face contemptuous. 'By God, Calvin! This is the first time that someone has bested you! And just at the time we need every fast gun we can get!'

'Put out the word out. They'll come in droves.'

'Aaaah!' The miner growled. 'We'll have every two-bit leather-slapper this side of the Rio coming in and wasting our time! We need men like Nevada – men who've proved themselves already! Instead, you've alienated him and now he's probably working *against* us – for Broken T!'

'He told me he wasn't gonna work for us, Kyle. I figured to throw a scare into him.' He smiled crookedly. 'He'll never beat me in a square-off, I can guarantee that.'

'You may very well have to,' snapped Harding, striding over to the window that overlooked the dusty yard and the broken rock on the endless belt that carried it to the stamp-mill. 'Nevada Hawk would've been a real asset. Now he's gone over to the enemy! Thanks to you!'

'I'll take a special interest in him, Kyle,' Judd said. 'Give it all I've got. You've no need to worry.'

Harding rounded swiftly at Judd's cocky tone. 'You think this is going to be a great chance for you to wage a private war against Nevada because he's dented your damn pride!'

Judd sobered, flushing a little. 'Well, he's dangerous and ought to be taken care of pronto.'

Harding nodded slowly. 'Yes, I agree with that. But you had your chance and muffed it!' He sighed heavily. 'I've had a letter from head office. They're climbing my back and standing on my shoulders! I went out on a limb when Jim Corey and that prospector he'd hired showed us samples of gold they claimed came from the ranchland. Now the stockholders, foreigners from Germany and Britain and Italy mostly, are clamouring to see their dividends improving out of sight!'

'They will – once we move the blasted ranchers!'

'They'd better!' Harding gritted. 'You know Amarosa doesn't mess about. They've ploughed thousands into this, on my say-so – it fails and my head's on the block. And if that happens, I assure you I'll have plenty of company!'

Judd frowned, secretly pleased to see his boss rattled this way. 'Step up the rough stuff then. Plenty of hardcases in town'll be happy to earn a dollar by kicking the butts of those cowboys. They wreck the town on their Saturday night wingdings. We can make sure that Nevada don't poke his nose in without it getting well and truly tweaked.'

Harding returned to his desk, tapped his long fingers against the oak edge. 'There's Hewitt.'

'*Hewitt*!' Judd almost spat on the floor as he said the sheriff's name. 'Judas, Kyle, that drunk doesn't even rate a mention.'

Harding didn't reply for some time and Judd frowned, wondering what he had missed. 'He's only token law, I give you that, but law nonetheless. If we had him on our side, backing the mine, it would count as a big advantage.'

Judd's frown deepened. 'Am I hearing right? You want to get Lang Hewitt on our side?' He flung out his arms. 'What the hell good would that do? The man lost his nerve years ago. He'll side with anyone who'll buy him a drink.'

Harding smiled crookedly as he raised his gaze to Judd's face. 'Sure. But s'pose he couldn't *find* anyone to pay for his drinks? Or supply him with rotgut whiskey?'

'What? Hell, he'd go crazy, swing from the chand-deliers, end up with the night terrors, clear off his head. . . .'

'. . . Or – do anything, *anything* he was told, just to get his hands on a glass of booze!' Harding let the words hang and Judd, his mouth partly open, a little thick blood oozing from the cut on his forehead gathering in his eyebrow unnoticed, stood there thinking about it. 'We can bring that kind of pressure to bear on Hewitt, Calvin. We have financial interests in the town's saloons. All we do is make it clear, *very* clear, that there would be drastic action taken against any man who supplied booze to our esteemed sher-iff. . . .'

Judd smiled slowly. 'By God, Kyle, I still don't know exactly what good it'll do to have Hewitt on our side – but if that's what you want, you've sure found the way to do it!'

CHAPTER 7

ROUGH STUFF

Predictably, Bo Whelan didn't roll out a red carpet or organize waving flags to welcome Nevada.

As soon as he could get Barbara alone he did so, coming into her ranch office with a stomping tread, slamming the door behind him. She looked up angrily from adding Nevada's name to her payroll.

'Oh, it's only you, Bo – with your usual spoilt brat entrance. You don't have to say a thing. I know why you're upset and on the prod.'

'Well, what you gonna do about it?' Bo was sweating, riled, his eyes seeming to have withdrawn deeply into their sockets so they were glittering pinpoints now. He leaned his big hands on the desk edge and Barbara sat back in her chair, arching her fine golden eyebrows.

'I don't intend to do anything about it. Nevada is now on the payroll, earning fighting pay from the moment I wrote his name down.'

Whelan glared. 'Why the hell you doin' this, Barbara? Your pa an' Ty got along OK with me takin' care of things. We don't need the likes of that drifter!'

'That's where you're wrong, Bo. We do need his kind of man. Desperately.' She held up a hand to stop the angry outburst she saw coming. 'We're living on our nerves all the time, virtually waiting for Harding to make his next move.'

'Hell, I've told you plenty of times, let me take some of the boys, and a few others I know livin' back in the hills, and we can hit that goddamn mine so hard, they'll think they've been through their own stamp-mill!'

'And I've always told you it's a stupid suggestion – the very thing that would bring the law down on us so quickly, we'd barely have time to draw breath.'

'Law? Thought we said we'd forget Hewitt, damnit!'

'You watch the way you talk!' Her face was tight with anger and he shuffled a little, nodded, mumbled something that might have been a half-hearted apology. Quietening down, she said: 'Amarosa won't mess with Hewitt! They'll bring in a federal marshal with full jurisdiction. The Territory of New Mexico has already applied for full statehood although it'll be sometime yet before it's admitted to the Union. But out-and-out lawlessness won't help, could jeopardize things, set it back many years. We'd be in more trouble than you can shake a stick at. And Amarosa work way above the level of Castle Rock. They even have Washington senators they call by their first names.'

'Aw! Don't bring politics into this, Barbara!'

'You fool, they're already there. It's why Amarosa can get away with riding roughshod over everyone who gets in their way. But it'll be a different kettle of fish if anything drastic happens to *them*! They pay *big* taxes, and they can bend the ears of all those senators I mentioned. Small-timers like us and Stoddart's Circle S wouldn't even get a hearing. They're sitting pretty and we'll have to knuckle under – for the time being. Understand?'

Bo tightened his mouth. 'Yeah, yeah, you've told me a couple dozen times—'

'Then it's about time it sunk in!'

'I didn't come in here to talk politics. I want to know just how much say this Nevada's got. And where do I stand!'

'You're still foreman of the Broken T.'

'I'm glad to hear it! So, Nevada takes orders from me like all the other rannies.' He broke off as she started to shake her head. He straightened, hands clenching down at his sides. 'What's that look for?'

'Nevada is a special case. He's a troubleshooter. and I emphasize the word *trouble*. He's responsible only to me, Bo.'

'Aw, the hell with this, Barbara! I've worked for you Tates for fifteen years! I don't deserve this kinda treatment.'

'Like everyone else, Bo, you can take it or leave it.'

Their gazes clashed and he frowned slightly. 'You fallen for this feller?'

The suggestion shocked her and for a moment she

was speechless. Then she began to chuckle, shaking her head again. 'Only you could think up such a thing, Bo! No, I haven't "fallen" for Nevada, as you put it. I'm an opportunist, Bo. I saw a chance to make use of Nevada Hawk and I took it. I want your co-operation, but if you won't give it, then you can draw your time. The way I've planned it, Nevada is going to be the salvation of Broken T and maybe all the basin ranches; not that I give much of a damn about *them*.'

He stepped back, glared, frowning deeply as he studied her beautiful face. 'Well, I dunno what you're gettin' at, but way I see things, it don't do much for me!'

She smiled, locking her hands behind her full head of blonde hair, smiling kind of secretly. 'You'll still be ramrod of the Broken T, long after Nevada Hawk has gone, Bo. Does that put your mind at rest?'

'Not by a damn sight – because, like I said, I don't savvy what you've got in mind!'

'I'm not revealing all my plans to you or anyone else, Bo! But I'll tell you this, and I'm sure it'll make you happy. Perhaps we should see if this Nevada is as good as I hope. So, if you want to test Nevada, kind of let him know that he can't interfere with your ranch decisions. . . .' She spread her hands, 'I'm not going to jump in and stop you. But you'll have to live with the outcome. I won't take sides.'

He had to absorb that for a minute, and then he grinned suddenly. 'Well, don't reckon you'll need too. It'll be mighty obvious who's the top man! Thanks, Barb, thanks a lot. I'll test him all right!'

He swung away and went out swiftly. Just for a moment she looked uncertain but then shrugged it off.

The more violent and unstable Nevada appeared, the better in the long run, she decided.

Bo Whelan picked his time: just as the men were assembling for supper under the big shingle-roofed dogrun that linked the house, kitchen and bunkhouse.

The cowboys were talking, some sluicing water over their sweaty faces at the wash-bench, others lounging; all of them were looking at Nevada.

He leaned a shoulder against an upright, finishing a cigarette, idly looking over the ranch hands. They seemed pretty much the usual mix: long, short and tall, fat and skinny, one or two middle-aged, the others mostly between early twenties and thirty. There were a dozen here but likely others still out on the range, overnighting on chores. He had had a couple of friendly nods by way of greeting, a couple of scowls, and a lot of puzzled, querying looks. They had no doubt heard all about his exploits with Corey-Ketchum and Lew Abbott, and labelled him a gunslinger, a *pistolero* for hire.

Now they were wondering what in hell he was doing rubbing shoulders with them.

Bo Whelan came swaggering in from the wash-bench, wiping his neck on a small, ragged piece of towel. He stopped in front of Nevada who glanced at him and nodded slightly.

'Get this straight, gunfighter. I'm the ramrod here.

The men take orders from me. If we're workin' cows and you're helpin', you take orders from me. If Barbara wants you to do a special chore, she'll tell you. At all other times you just *stay the hell outta my way*! You got it?'

'Old Deaf Baldy in the next county could get it the way you're yelling,' Nevada told him and immediately the buzz of talk stopped and all gazes turned to the foreman. Nevada, who hadn't moved, was still smoking down his cigarette. *The clash had to come sometime; might as well get it over with.* . . .

Bo glared, then his thick lips tightened a little and he said quietly, 'Forgot to mention. No one on the payroll, no one, sasses me!'

He flicked with the towel and the ragged, wet end caught Nevada on the left cheek, cracking like the thong of a quirt. His head jerked back and he staggered away from the post. The moment he had balance he flicked his burning cigarette into Bo's smirking face. The man yelled, slapping it away in a shower of sparks. By then Nevada's right fist was crossing over, a short blow, but travelling fast and hard. It hooked Bo on the side of the jaw and sent him sprawling into the group of men who were closing in swiftly, sensing some pre-meal entertainment coming up.

Rough hands grasped the falling ramrod and he cursed as he was helped to his feet and thrust back towards Nevada, who was standing with one hand down at his side, the other rubbing the red mark on his cheek. He waited and Bo Whelan grinned, spat a little blood-flecked spittle to the side.

'Guess there's only one way you're gonna savvy who really runs things around here, drifter!'

Nevada still said nothing and Bo charged in, big fists cocked, shoulder muscles bunched, eyes narrowed and glittering with eager anticipation of inflicting pain.

Nevada parried the first three blows and saw that this gave Whelan pause; he hadn't expected that. Likely most times he cut loose with a flurry of blows the other man went down bleeding. This time his fists were slapped aside and then he glimpsed Nevada's deadpan face for an instant before the top of the man's head smashed into his already swollen and bruised nose. Whelan staggered and flailed, blood spread in ragged lines across his face, his lips mashed against teeth that creaked in his gums.

The cowboys opened out, blinking at this unexpected turn; not without some pleasure, either, as every one of them had felt Bo's fists over the time they had worked for Broken T. Nevada strode forward purposefully, but without hurry, caught a fistful of Bo's hair and as the man's hands instinctively grasped his wrists, yanked his head up. A clubbing left hammered down and Whelan shuddered as it landed and almost broke his jaw. The impact wrenched him free of the grip on his greasy hair and he fell to one knee. Nevada gave him one of his own knees in the chest and stretched him out on the gritty floorboards.

Bo was hurt and bleeding, but he was a tough man. While most would have either played possum to avoid further punishment, or passed out, he grabbed the post beside him and hauled himself upright. He didn't let go of the post, clung to it, took his weight on his hands and swung his legs up as Nevada closed.

The gunfighter took both boots in the chest, high up, just under his jaw. The pain contorted his face and he gagged, fighting for a breath. Bo launched himself, his own face a mask of blood, rage driving him. Both arms flailed and he set his boots firmly, grunted with each hammering blow, not allowing Nevada a second to recover. The troubleshooter went down to one knee, then fell sideways. The first boot skidded off his ribs but the second landed solidly enough to move his bulk at least a foot across the boardwalk under the dogrun. The men scattered to make room as he rolled in an effort to escape further punishment. Bo was cursing aloud as he stomped in, boots swinging mercilessly, blood-smeared teeth bared, the light of pleasure brightening his deepset eyes. Nevada brought up short against the lower legs of the yelling men before they had time to jump back. He instantly used this slight bracing of his body by reaching up, grabbing Bo's descending boot in both hands and digging in his own heels as he thrust backwards with his powerful legs.

The movement pulled Whelan off balance and he danced on one leg so as to stay upright. Nevada lifted his legs and drove his boots into Bo's knees. The ramrod moaned and tumbled, the motion wrenching his foot out of Nevada's grip. The gunfighter rolled and got to his feet, slowly, for he had been hurt, and swayed before he started after Bo. The man was still bent over and Nevada chopped him with two punches, left and right, sending the ramrod staggering away from the dogrun and into the ranch yard. As he fought to stay on his feet, Nevada moved after him relentlessly. Bo saw him coming, staggered towards the corrals and turned with his back to the rails suddenly. But Nevada hadn't run after him, simply kept striding in as if he would walk clear through the man and the corral fence, too.

It unnerved Bo as he gathered his spinning senses: no one had stood up to his punishment before this. He usually laid out his opponents in a few minutes, without taking more than a blow or two himself. Now he knew what it felt like to be hammered and butted and kicked – and he didn't like it. But he was mighty aware that he was facing one of his toughest tests now. He couldn't go down to this goddamn ranny, not in front of the cowhands – and Barbara, who was watching from a front window, discreetly holding a corner of the lace curtain aside to get a clearer view.

Bitch! She had set him up for this!

It was the trigger to renewed anger and determination and he suddenly thrust off the corral rails, hooking a boot-heel over the bottom pole, adding impetus to his thrusting body. Nevada saw the man hurtling at him and stepped to one side but not quite fast enough. Bo, well-versed in rough-and-tumble brawling, simply threw an arm out to that side and it caught Nevada on the ear.

Head ringing, Nevada floundered and while he was off balance, Bo leapt in, arms blurring like pistons as he whipped a flurry of punches into

Nevada. The man stumbled, covering instinctively, but he had to keep moving now so as to maintain what little balance he had left. Then his shoulder crashed against an angle of the corral fence and the jar shook him. He hit his head on the top lodgepole and stars spun behind his eyes. Dazed, he felt hard fists jarring him as Bo, teeth bared in a tight grin now, set himself and began driving home bone-cracking blows in a monotony of repetition, fists landing on the same spot over and over, doing a lot of damage, shaking Nevada's entire body.

Nevada felt himself fading now; his legs were starting to creak and fold under him. He grabbed at the rail with his left hand – then suddenly swung his weight from that hand, managing to dodge Bo's next swing. The fist grazed his battered ribs, but Nevada's whole body was twisting towards Bo now and his right fist whistled as he brought it down off the top rail. There was a crack and Whelan's head snapped back on his neck. He flew back several feet, boots scrabbling for a solid hold, staring up into the sundown sky with eyes that were full of pain – and a sudden knowledge that he wasn't going to win this fight.

Hell! He'd be lucky to even walk away from this hell-on-wheels ranny boring into him!

Adrenalin surged at the thought, but it came too late. Nevada Hawk strode in, fighting his legs that wanted to give way and let him fall, grabbed Bo's dirty, torn shirt-front and held him there. Bo's head was hanging limply and he felt too weak to lift aching, throbbing arms as Nevada looked down into the bloody face – and batted him back and forth with his open hand, back and forth, back and forth, smashing Bo's head side to side. Blood and a tooth flew, sweat sprayed from the man's hair and stung Nevada's eyes. But he kept on batting away, Bo's cheeks crunching against his teeth, the man's mouth full of blood so that he started to choke and cough. He sagged in Nevada's grip but the gunfighter kept hitting him, allowing him only to sink to his knees, that big, solid hand swinging ruthlessly.

Then, panting, weaving on unsteady legs, he stood before the beaten ramrod, moved behind him and placed a boot between the man's shoulders. He thrust once and Bo Whelan smashed face first into the ground, coughing and spluttering, his body convulsing, until, suddenly, he was still.

There wasn't a sound in the ranch yard except Nevada's heavy breathing. He turned and stumbled to the horse-trough, dropping to his knees as he reached aching, swollen hands into the straw-flecked water and splashed some into his battered face.

At the front window, Barbara slowly let the curtain fall back into place. She continued to stare out through the lace, breathing quite hard, seeing a blurred view of the yard and what was happening out there.

There wasn't much at the moment. A few of the cowhands were tentatively moving towards Bo Whelan's prostrate body. Nobody ventured near Nevada, who was still monotonously splashing his face and head with water.

She smiled faintly. A beating wouldn't go astray for Bo: it would be a new experience for him. He was a bully and a brute at best of times. But he had met his match now. It had worked out well, though she was a little worried.

Both had fought hard and she knew she would be short of two good men for a day or two. She hoped Harding wouldn't make any drastic moves against Broken T in that time, for she wouldn't have much to fight with. The cowhands, promised a bonus if there was trouble, still weren't eager to tangle with Amarosa hardcases.

She hurried into the office and took the ranch journal down from the shelf behind her desk. It was heavy, leather-bound and scarred, and had recorded Broken T's history from the first day her father had bought the land and started to build up the spread. She turned to the current page, dipped a pen in the clay inkwell and wrote the day's date. After pausing thoughtfully for a moment, she wrote underneath:

Bad brawl today between Bo Whelan and new man, a gunfighter named Nevada; they hate each other and maybe enough to kill. I hope I haven't made a mistake in hiring such a brutal man but I need someone like him to help me in the long fight with Amarosa. Tho' I fear he's more a troublemaker than troubleshooter!

There! That was just the way she wanted it to read.

Anyone checking the journal – and there could come a time when she would be glad that someone did – they would see for themselves that she had had reservations about hiring a man like Nevada, but was desperate enough to chance it.

Blaming him for starting the brawl with Bo Whelan would add weight to her innocent plea when she insisted she had no idea he would be so violent and dangerous, even going so far as to spark all-out war between Amarosa and the ranches of the basin. . . .

Barbara smiled. 'Ooh, you're downright sneaky, girl! Your father would be proud of you!'

CHAPTER 8

NIGHT RIDERS

One man stood just outside the door of the line shack, holding a rifle low down across his belly, while the second remained out of sight inside. But there were the long double barrels of a shotgun poking under the shutter to one side of the door. There was a small garden, flowers mixed in with a few vegetables, behind a low white picket border-fence along the front of the cabin.

The one with the rifle was young, early twenties, looked a little reckless and vague to Nevada as he put his horse up the slope leading to the cabin.

'Who you?' called the young rifleman, his voice thin but not in anyway afraid.

'Nevada. New man. Barbara sent me up.'

The youngster, squinted, head on one side. 'Looks like she oughta sent a sawbones with you.' He sniggered, turned his head towards the shutter. 'Ollie. C'mon out here and take a look at this feller. Looks like a hog gnawed on his face!'

Nevada stopped the horse, folded his hands on the saddle horn. The shotgun withdrew beneath the shutter and then Ollie appeared with the weapon held casually down at his side. The other man had his rifle dangling, too.

Both jumped and paled when Nevada suddenly moved his right hand and held his cocked Colt on them. 'Boys, you gotta keep your wits about you. Don't get distracted or you could end up dead. I was you, I'd remember that.'

They were holding their breaths and now, wide-eyed, breathed away, licking their lips, Ollie having wet bright-red ones that gave his face a feminine appearance. The way he moved, too, had a woman's look: his hair was long and soft.

'Relax. You get that lesson for free.' Nevada smiled faintly as he spoke, but he didn't holster the revolver, although he let the barrel sag away from the young men a little. 'You'd be Ollie and Beege Westaway, I guess. Distant cousins, according to Barbara Tate.'

They were silent, exchanged glances and half-smiles and the rifleman, Beege, snickered. 'Not kissin' cousins, though!'

They both chuckled, pushing at each other with their elbows and Nevada frowned a little. He wasn't sure these two weren't kissing cousins the way they were behaving, especially Ollie, who was flapping his hands about a lot in what looked to Nevada like womanish gestures.

Well, it was nothing to do with him – or he hoped it wouldn't be, seeing as he was to stay here for a spell.

He knew Barbara had sent him up here mainly to separate him from Bo Whelan who had taken to his bunk, eyes swollen shut, face black and blue and rainbow-hued, pride very fragile – and mighty unforgiving.

As for Nevada, he didn't care much one way or the other; if Bo wanted to continue the fight, maybe escalate it to guns, he would oblige the man. Just as easily he would shake the ramrod's hand and let their brawl fade into the past. It was all up to Bo. But for now he had line-camp duty.

The Westaways invited him inside, made coffee and served up biscuits that were quite fresh. When Nevada remarked on it, Ollie drew himself up an extra inch or so and bowed slightly, dusting off his small hands.

'Why, thank'ee, sir. 'Tis with me own hands that I made 'em.' And he made a small curtsy which brought a frown to Nevada's face.

Beege – they had already told him that the name came from the youth's initials: 'B-J', standing for Bradford Jonathan – laughed and snorted. 'Ain't he a character! But cooks a mean meal, Nevada, works genu-ine miracles with lard an' flour and a handful of raisins. Give him some apples and – man! – you ain't never gonna taste an apple-pie like he can whip up!'

'Sounds like I might even put on a pound or two while I'm up here,' Nevada remarked, sipping the coffee, which was also good and strong and flavoursome. 'Yeah. Reckon I'm gonna like it here.'

The Westaways exchanged looks of concern. 'Er –

how long you gonna stay?' Beege asked and Nevada could see that Ollie was hanging anxiously on his reply, too.

Seemed to him like he was going to be in the way with these two. 'Guess until the Tate woman calls me back or gives me another chore.'

'Well, why did you come here?' Beege asked and Ollie began self-consciously clearing away the things, straightening the edges of the gingham table-cloth that covered the old, scarred, deal table. The entire interior of the cabin was neat and tidy, way beyond anything Nevada had seen outside of a new bride's cottage; there was even a curtain on one window, the one above what turned out to be Ollie's bunk.

'She's afraid the Amarosa people might make a move against this camp. It's borderline with Broken T and the mine's outermost lease. She feels Harding would be happier if this wasn't manned by Broken T crew who could see what he's about.'

That really upset the cousins. They were edgy and dancing from one foot to the other. Ollie dropped a plate which shattered and he snapped 'Oh, bother!' and stomped outside in such a way that Nevada figured if he was wearing skirts he would have flounced them and hitched them up in frustration.

'You boys enjoy it up here? Away from the others?'

Beege glowered: *the protector*. 'What's that mean?' he snapped. 'You sayin' somethin'?'

Nevada spread his hands. 'Asked a simple question is all. What're you getting so flummoxed for? Hell, I don't care what you and Ollie get up to; that's your business. Just don't ever make the mistake of trying to get me to join in or your faces are gonna look a damn site worse than mine right now.'

Beege continued to glare. Then he drew in a deep breath and released it, nodding jerkily. 'There's a snug corner in that small storehouse and half-root-cellar we built – if you'd prefer to sleep there.'

'Anywhere that I find comfortable, I'll try it. It don't suit, you two can move out and I'll stay here.'

'Hey, wait up!'

Nevada gave him a deliberately cold look. 'Take it or leave it, friend. I'm not here for a discussion.'

'Are – are you here to make trouble with the mine people?'

'Not make it. But stop it if it comes our way.'

Beege nodded slowly. 'OK. Then Ollie an' me just . . . carry on as usual? Do our chores and . . . so on?'

Nevada smiled. 'If that's what you want to call it, sure. Just . . . carry on . . . carryin' on.'

He was surprised that Beege had the grace to blush.

He believed it was a nightmare.

Gunshots, shouting, at the edge of his conscious-ness. Eventually there were screams and dancing flames, horses, and men calling to each other, more gunshots and splintering timber.

Sweating, nauseous, he tossed and turned on the potato sacks he had piled against the rear wall of the little storehouse down the western slope below the line-camp. It had been built here to catch the cooler breezes, and sacks of food and vegetables and haunches of smoked venison and wild pork hung from hooks under the rafters. The whole place smelled like a root cellar, except it was mostly above ground – about three feet was below ground level – and this helped in the preservation of the supplies, too.

Nevada's bunk was against the rear earthen wall, the upper three feet of which was formed by small-diameter logs. Above these came the shingled roof. Feeling terrible, his head pounding, he seemed only half-conscious as he rolled about on the sacking, living this nightmare, groaning. He wanted to get up, douse his head in some cold creek-water in an effort to clear it, but he couldn't seem to move his limbs. They were leaden, as in those dreams when a man is trying to run from terrible danger but finding he gets nowhere or is unable to move at all as the danger hastens towards him. . . .

'Lemme . . . out!' he croaked, but fell back on his sacks. *God it was hot in here!* There was a roaring in his head now, the sound punctuated by more scattered gunfire, and it came to him that maybe he wasn't dreaming this at all – *that it was actually happening!* Outside the door!

'Good grief! Night-riders! A raid!'

He seemed to scream the words like a revelation but they were only inside his head. He was still unable to move his leaden limbs and now he smelled wood smoke – and saw fire reaching down to him from above.

He was rising into Hell! No, wait! That was wrong – you went down *into Hell, up to Heaven – that was what all the preachers said. . . .*

He shook his head, scattering his thoughts. Judas, he hadn't thought along those lines since he was a kid – but Ellie was a believer and he had tried not to disturb her too much by his cynicism. *That was long, long ago, you damn fool!*

But, for a moment, he had a wild thought: if he was on the verge of dying, did that mean he would soon see her again, and . . . ?

'Aaaagh!' He shouted this time, a loud, gravelly denial of such foolishness, but he tore away the mists that were shrouding his brain and even his vision, forced himself to roll off his pile of potato sacks and sprawled on all fours on the packed-earth floor. His head hung and sweat dripped on to the backs of his spread hands. His mouth was full of fur and bitter-tasting bile. He spat but it was no more than a frothy ball. Breathing was hard and his throat rasped. Raw smoke made him cough and hack, his lungs feeling as if they were tearing loose from his ribs.

Then the roof began to fall in. First, individual blazing shingles tumbled down, briefly lighting the interior of the storeroom. Beyond the angled trap-door entrance he could see more flames through the cracks in the warped timber. Shadows flitted like ghosts across the narrow gaps. Next, the rafters supporting the meat and foodsacks burned through and fell, one pinning him across the backs of his legs before he kicked free. Then he retched and lost the fine supper Ollie had cooked for him. Well, not for him, really – he had seen the exchanges of looks between the two cousins all day long, saw the brief, covert touching of hands as they passed, the rolling of eyes. He had figured these two had something special on this night so he had reckoned to quit the cabin early. Maybe he was a bit strait-laced, and didn't approve of that kind of relationship between males, but it was not his business and in every other way they seemed good ranch hands and human beings. He had been here a week now and they had taken to him all right, appreciated his non-interference; the rich supper had likely been a token of this appreciation as much as for their own benefit.

Anyway, he had enjoyed the meal, though the roast venison was a touch too spicy for him, but the vegetables were cooked to perfection and the raisin-duff went down well with cream separated and whipped personally by Ollie himself. (*He really should have been a woman, that kid!*) Maybe the coffee was a shade stronger than usual, a little too much on the bitter side, but he had drunk way, way worse.

'Obliged for the elegant meal, gents,' he had said, meaning it, as he rubbed his somewhat unsettled and slightly bloated stomach. 'If you don't mind, I'm tuckered from that long ride through the hills today, so I'll turn in early and leave you two to . . . amuse yourselves. Oh, damn! It's my turn to wash up the dishes, ain't it?'

'Nah, man, you do look tired, Nevada,' Beege said quickly. 'We'll do the dishes. You go turn in. . . .'

Which he had done – and had had those wild dreams and awakened to this living nightmare around him, feeling so queasy that he had begun to wonder whether, after all, there had been something not quite right with that elegant supper.

Now he wrenched himself back to reality. He

picked up his war bag and used it to batter away falling shingles, grabbed his gunbelt and Winchester and crawled towards the now blazing trap-door. Using the canvas war bag as a shield over his head, he charged up the three wooden steps and smashed his shoulders into the burning planks. They cracked and splintered and spun away and he sprawled out into the night, gasping, gagging, clothes smouldering. He rolled about in the grass to kill any incipient flames, keeping an instinctive grip on his guns.

The ground had been churned up by the hoofs of at least a half-dozen riders.

His body slid down the slope a ways and when he stopped, he wrenched around, looked back, head spinning, thundering with noise that was all inside his skull.

The cabin was no more than a blazing skeleton of blackened, flame-edged frame timbers. There was the crack of a shot and he ducked as it was followed by a shotgun blast, then several more cracks from a rifle or pistol.

But it was only stored ammunition in the cabin exploding with the heat. He lay prone, hugging the ground, watching the line-camp burn down, knowing that no one could possibly still be alive in there.

No one!

At the same time he smelled the sickening odour of charred meat and his churning belly heaved again.

After that he pressed his hot face into the coolness of the grass and felt waves of oblivion washing over him.

CHAPTER 9

DEBTS

Half-way down the slope Nevada was met by a band of sweating, armed riders led by Calvin Judd.

Their guns were all trained on the battered and dishevelled Nevada. He reined up, saw it was no use reaching for any of his weapons, sat holding the reins loosely, hands where they could be seen. He swayed in the saddle, not so much fatigued as mighty woozy in the head; he kept wanting to fall sideways and had consciously to fight to stay upright in the saddle.

Judd put his horse forward and slowly walked it around the smoke-smelling man. He rode in close enough to poke Nevada hard in the ribs with the barrel of his carbine. Nevada winced and tightened his grip on the reins, almost falling. He swivelled reddened eyes that were still slightly out of focus to the mining man. 'What're you doing here?'

'We saw the fire, smelled the smoke – and look at what we found!' Judd put on an overplayed puzzled look, swivelling his gaze towards his own men. 'Actually, men, what *have* we found? Anyone recognize it?' He poked with the carbine again and Nevada was hard put to stay mounted. 'Looks like something the cat threw up in the alley back of the saloon to me. What say you fellers?'

'Nigra who's had a damn good wash in our run-off?' suggested one dark-skinned, hard-faced character in a dirty pink-and-white checked shirt. 'Done it in streaks, but! Like a goddamn piebald!'

That brought a laugh from the Amarosa crew and even Calvin Judd allowed himself a small, crooked smile.

'Not bad, Jaybird, not bad at all. For a 'breed. But maybe he's just a drunken buck from the reservation, who fell in the creek. You believe these whining ranchers, it reeks of run-off. That could account for this one's stink.'

He prodded again and this time Nevada fell – half-fell – tried hard to grab at the horn, slowed a little but still sprawled awkwardly. He clung to the stirrup as Judd rode closer and cracked the carbine barrel across his knuckles. When he let go of the stirrup iron he fell on his face, half-under his mount, which shied away with a snort.

Judd nudged his own mount forward and Nevada, not really fully conscious, had to roll and slew and scrabble aside to avoid being trodden on. Calvin Judd leaned down and spat on him.

'I think we might just put you out of your misery, Mr Whoever-you-are!' He levered a shell into the carbine's breech and a couple of the watching men moved uncomfortably in their saddles. The one called Jaybird cleared his throat, bringing Judd's cold gaze around to him smartly.

'Easy, Cal! Harding never meant us to go that far!'

Judd's frosty stare held to the 'breed and then the carbine swung up and he triggered it one-handed. Jaybird slapped a hand to his face, shouting as he reeled in his saddle. Blood ran between his fingers and he moved the hand to clamp his bloody ear. The bullet had seared his cheek, then clipped his ear, cutting a notch the size of a dime.

'Hey! For Chris'sake, Cal! What the hell're you doin'?'

Judd put the smoking rifle on the man again. 'You have been told a hundred times how I am to be addressed, Jaybird! Now tell me instantly how you should do it – or my next bullet will go through the middle of your ugly face!'

'I – I'm sorry, *Mr* Judd! Just a – a slip of the lip!' the 'breed gasped, half-cowering, in expectation of receiving another of Judd's bullets.

The gunfighter nodded curtly. 'You remember that "Mister".' He lowered the carbine, looked down at Nevada who was obviously less conscious than previously. 'Well, I suppose I'd better not shoot this . . . thing right now, but. . . .'

'Aw, go ahead, Judd! We'd love to witness a cold-blooded murder done by you!'

The group had been so involved in their own little drama that they hadn't heard the second bunch of riders coming. There were at least ten, outnumbering the Amarosa crew by four, and their guns were all cocked and ready for action. The mine group backed off, sheathed their rifles, some lifting hands out to the side. Only Judd retained his carbine and he glared now at Bo Whelan at the head of his cowhands.

'I wondered what had happened to Nevada's face. Now I can see you two have had a difficulty.' Judd bared his teeth coldly. 'I'm glad to see you came off second best, Whelan!'

'I'll even that score when I'm ready,' Bo said in clipped tones. 'How'd *you* do when you met Nevada? I hear you missed your footin' on a flight of stairs, huh. . . ?'

Judd scowled. 'We'll be on our way.'

'When we say so!' Bo snapped, stopping the mine crew as they lifted their reins. 'You're on Broken T land here. Trespassin'.'

Judd smiled bleakly. 'Just being neighbourly. We spotted the fire in your line-camp and rode across to see if we could do anything to help . . . Right, men?'

Naturally, the scowling Jaybird and the others emphatically agreed. Bo Whelan seemed uncertain for a moment and then jerked his rifle. 'Go on then – git! An' stay git! You cross over on to Broken T again and you'll go back on a plank.'

The group was already moving and Bo ordered four armed men to follow to make sure they cleared Broken T. Meantime, he dismounted beside Nevada and lifted him to a sitting position. Nevada's head lolled on his neck and Bo sent two men up to examine the burned-out shell of the line-camp as he shook Nevada. The man slurred something unintelligible.

102

'He ain't got any bad wounds that I can see, but he sure is half-way outta things. By God! If he ain't hurt he's gotta be damn well drunk!' Bo announced and grinned. 'Barb is gonna love this!'

'He smell of booze, Bo?' one rider asked and earned a savage look.

'Help me get him back on his hoss, and tie him in the saddle. I want him back at Broken T pronto so's Barb can see just what a hotshot she's gone an' hired!'

'He's not drunk,' Barbara Tate said with a touch of relief in her voice as she straightened from examining Nevada as he lay stretched out on the bed in the ranch's spare room. 'But there's a peculiar odour on his breath that I recognize. Ty broke his collar-bone once and Doc Martell said he would have to set it, but the pain would be very severe. He had no morphine so he used something else – drops from a bottle. I can almost see the label . . . Ah, yes! Chloral hydrate! The doctor actually laughed and said it was what they used on the 'Frisco docks to knock out men they wanted to shanghai for the schooners on the China run. They slipped it into their drinks. He called it a "Mickey Finn".'

Bo Whelan frowned. 'I dunno what you're sayin' . . .'

'I'm saying that someone slipped Nevada a Mickey Finn! Knocked him out with chloral hydrate!'

'Who the hell would want to do that? Ah! Musta been them crazy kids up at the line-camp. I heard they experimented with opium once. Ollie was outta his head for days.'

'I recall. Yes! It might well have been the Westaways but . . . we'll never know now, for sure.'

She sobered, thinking of the dead youths, distant kin, burned beyond recognition up at the line-camp. She shuddered a little, turned to Bo. 'I'll get him cleaned up and bandaged. It's very lucky that he wasn't killed, too!' Her face was hard and Bo shrugged.

'Guess he was sleepin' out in the storeroom. Yeah, lucky sonuver, all right.' There was no real sympathy in his voice or in the look on his battered face. He had no love for the big man sprawled unconscious on the bed. It had taken four, almost five, days for the swelling around Bo's eyes to subside enough for him even to begin to see. Longer for the body pains to go away. But it would take a damn sight longer yet for him to forget what Nevada had done to him in front of the Broken T crew.

That would have to wait, though; right now there was work to be done. 'I better get some of the boys cleanin' up that line-camp before Judd makes a move on it,' he said. She nodded, frowning, as he went out hurriedly.

She turned back to Nevada who was moaning a little now, and carefully began to peel the charred clothing from his suffering body.

At least she had proof now that Harding was increasing the pressure on Broken T . . . if anyone should ask.

And she would make sure they did.

Nevada's burns were relatively minor but the headache

was about the worst he could remember ever experiencing. Several times he felt for the tomahawk he was sure was buried in his skull, slicing into his brain, mangling the nerves. One of these times his involuntary moans brought Barbara Tate hurrying in.

'It's your head, isn't it?' She didn't wait for his reply. 'It's to be expected. The doctor told me chloral hydrate leaves you with a very severe headache that can last for days.'

'Coral – who?' slurred Nevada, squinting in the sunlight streaming in the window, only now realizing that he must be in the Broken T ranch house.

She explained briefly about the potent knock-out drug. 'It must have been the Westaway boys.'

He frowned and even that small movement made him grunt. 'Now why would they KO me? We got along all right. I left 'em to . . . whatever they wanted to do. . . .' He paused, nodded very gently. 'Oh, yeah. That could be it.' He looked at her closely. 'You know about them boys? I mean, Ollie shoulda been a gal, and . . .' He trailed off, feeling himself blushing, not able to find the words to explain to Barbara that the Westaways had been homosexuals.

Showing some embarrassment she nodded, tight-lipped. 'I heard rumours from the bunkhouse. I never enquired too deeply into it. They were good ranch hands, never bothered anyone and did their job well. That's all I asked.'

'That's right. But I figure they had something kind of special on last night and wanted to make sure I didn't interrupt, or something.' He felt tongue-tied again, added in a rush: 'So they cooked me a slap-up meal and they could've put some kinda drug in my food or coffee – which tasted queer – just to make sure I didn't bother 'em.'

She sighed, nodding. 'I think that's what happened, too. You probably feel as terrible as you look right now, but it will wear off. You need rest and lots of coffee.'

'It embarrasses me some to tell you that right now, I'd be glad of both.'

'Then I'll see you get those things. Did you see who raided the line-camp?'

'No. The drug worked well. When I came round – *half*-round, everything was on fire. I was lucky to get out of that storeroom. The raiders had long gone by then and I wasn't in a fit state to look around much. Just made sure I couldn't help the Westaways. I wouldn't've been much help anyway, I guess. But Calvin Judd and some of his men waylaid me down the slope. So – how did I get here?'

She told Nevada about Bo Whelan's group, on their way to the line-camp fire, coming across Judd and his riders.

Despite the pain, Nevada hung up each eyebrow in a high arch. 'You're not telling me Bo saved my life?'

'I believe he did.'

'Man, I bet that hurt!'

She smiled crookedly. 'I dare say. I'll get you some strong coffee. And then I – I'll have to ride into town and arrange a funeral for the Westaways. I owe them that.'

'I'd like to see 'em buried decent. . . .'

'I doubt if the preacher will want to give them

106

Christian burial,' she said worriedly and then saw the sudden hardness square the angles on his battered face, still marked with smears of charcoal.

'He'll do it,' was all he said and she knew she needn't worry about that part any more.

Even beat-up and battered like this, Nevada Hawk was a comforting man to have around. *If he was on your side!*

No one could tell that there was anything much wrong with Nevada when he rode into town on the day of the funeral and stopped off at the small Episcopalian church on the north side of the town's plaza. Sure, he looked bruised and blistered around the face and one of his hands had burns on the back and he limped a little, but he moved around pretty good.

And Preacher Dodd swallowed his pride in the face of Nevada's cold stare and the even colder and blacker stare of the muzzle of his Colt, and agreed to read over the charred remains of the Westaway boys from the Bible.

It was predictably a small funeral; only a few townsfolk turned up, most of them only curious, and a representative group from the Broken T crew. Some of Harding's men were in town and a couple stood around under the cottonwoods at the edge of Boot Hill. They didn't even remove their hats as the preacher said his words, hurried away after sprinkling a little dirt on the cheap coffins that had been lowered into a single grave.

Barbara didn't cry but she was very quiet and sober, perhaps her eyes glinting a little more than

107

usual. She took Nevada's arm, surprising him, and when he realized that she was going to hold on until they got back into town proper, he made her change over to his left side, keeping his gun arm free.

'You're a careful man, Nevada.' She waited for a reply but received nothing, not even a grunt. 'Head feeling better?'

'Just about feel like I'm walking on the ground again. I'll go have a beer before I ride back. OK with you?'

He handed her up into her buggy where one of the Mexican roustabouts, choking in his best clothes, sat in the driving-seat. Then he sauntered across to the saloon and, inside, found Sheriff Lang Hewitt in an argument with the man behind the bar.

'Who the hell says I can't buy a bottle of rye if I want it? I can pay, damnit!'

'I can't do it, Sheriff,' the saloon man said, uncomfortably. 'I – been told you ain't to be supplied with any hard likker.'

'Who the *hell* told you that?' stormed Hewitt.

'The owners. An' no use askin' me who that is, 'cause there's half a dozen of 'em got shares in this place. I want to stay in business, I gotta do what they say. Sorry, Lang.'

Hewitt had the shakes, Nevada could see that, and the man was taken off guard by the news that he wouldn't be able to buy whiskey to steady him down. He seemed to be trying hard to make a decision on what to do about it.

'Lang, someone's got it in for you,' the saloon man said in a low voice. 'There's been a warnin' that anyone gives you hard likker, they get the bejesus beat outta them – or worse. I think by Calvin Judd.'

Hewitt stiffened, his puzzled frown deepening. 'What the hell. . . ? Who said *that*, for Chris'sakes?'

The barkeep rubbed hard at the shotglasses he was cleaning on a grey piece of towel and without looking up, and moving his lips hardly at all, said: 'B'lieve it was Calvin hisself. . . .'

Hewitt's once square, wide shoulders, sagged in an even more round-backed shape than usual. 'Aw, shoot!' The sheriff pushed back off the bar, face tight now. 'I-I gotta see about this!' He turned to swing away and collided with Nevada, who reached out to steady the man.

'Easy, Lang. How about a beer?'

Hewitt snorted. 'You been standin' there long enough to hear what Earl said.' He jerked a head towards the barkeep and Nevada looked steadily at the man. 'They won't serve me!'

'I heard him say you couldn't have any *hard* liquor. That don't mean beer.' He lowered his voice as he turned the not-so-reluctant sheriff towards the bar. 'There's enough alcohol in it to help ease the heebie-jeebies, Lang.'

Hewitt leaned on the bar. 'How the hell would you know?'

'Been there. After Ketchum killed my wife. Found out after a few weeks, boozing was no answer to what ailed me. So I set out to track down Ketchum and his gang. . . .'

Nevada signalled impatiently to Earl. The man hesitated a few moments more, then drew a large glass of frothing beer. 'Make it two,' Nevada said.

Hewitt tapped fingers rapidly on the zinc edge of the bar until Earl set the glass before him. Then he grabbed it in both hands and glugged it down, spilling some down his neck and shirt-front. He smacked froth-edged lips as he set down the glass. Nevada had been about to drink from the second beer but when he saw the state Hewitt was in – getting worse as his brain began fully to realize what the ban on whiskey meant – he handed the sheriff his glass. Hewitt grabbed it and drank it down as fast as the first, drew the back of a now steadier hand across his lips, nodded thanks.

'You're a queer one, Nevada – but thanks. An', between you an' me, the reason I drink ain't because some scum killed my wife. I was the one done the killin'!'

Nevada took his arm. 'Come over to a corner table, Lang. And you bring another two beers, Earl.'

Seated, now sipping his third beer, Hewitt pursed his lips and said: 'Was a trail herd in Kansas done it. Cowpokes drove it down Main after I told 'em to go round the town. Tryin' me on, see. I was ragin' at the trail boss defyin' me that way and I never thought; I just reached for my gun and they reached for theirs and we shot it out. I killed two, winged a third, caught one myself alongside the head.' He touched his temple above his left ear and Nevada thought he saw fading scar tissue there. Hewitt swallowed and his voice cracked. 'By then, the gunfire'd caused a stampede – them trail-spooked, half-starved steers wrecked Main and most of its storefronts. Injured seven people. Killed two, both kids. . . .'

His voice trailed off and he downed the rest of his beer in one large gulp. Nevada said nothing, pushed his own partly drunk beer across. Hewitt's hands were shaking when he picked it up.

He suddenly paused, squinted at Nevada. 'Don't think that buyin' me a couple beers is gonna get you off the hook.'

Warily, Nevada asked, 'What hook's that?'

Hewitt couldn't put it off any longer, drank half the big glass, wiped his mouth again. 'The one I was on my way to see you about.'

'Yeah, I noticed you were all ready for the trail.'

Hewitt sat up straighter. 'Don't sass me, you lousy gunslinger! I told you to quit my town and I hear you been raisin' all kindsa hell out at the mines and in the valley.' He swallowed and pointed a slightly trembly finger. 'You – is a troublemaker, feller, an' I don't want you in my bailiwick.'

'You know what happened or just going on what you been told?'

'Well – what I been told. But I was gonna 'vestigate! Damn right I was! It's my – my dooty.' He smiled, a tight movement of his mouth but without much humour in it. He lowered his voice. 'You an' a lotta others are makin' a big mistake about me.'

'How about you set me right then?'

'Huh! You just stick aroun' and see for y'self, mister.' He winked ponderously. 'Just 'cause a man does a little extra drinkin' and gets drunk, don't mean he's lost his nerve completely – and that's the big mistake you an the others've made! Thinkin' I'm

111

gutless 'cause I booze.'

He nodded several times, convincing himself as much as Nevada. He had to get both hands on the beer-glass this time to drink and Nevada knew beer wasn't going to do it with Hewitt. He needed a shot or two of the hard stuff to really steady him up.

While the sheriff drank down the beer, Nevada went to the bar, spoke to Earl in a low voice. The man jumped back, shaking his head. 'I dasn't do that! Calvin Judd would come in here and burn me out!'

'Why? You haven't supplied any hard liquor to Hewitt – *I'm* the one buying. And what *I* do with it is my own business.'

'Why the hell you feedin' him rotgut?'

'I want him to feel better than he does right now. He's getting ready to do what he sees as his duty and damned if I'll see him ride off half-way into the terrors just because he can't get a decent drink to brace him up.'

Earl studied him for a long moment. 'I gotta say that this ain't what I expected from you. Not after what I heard about you.'

'Never listen to gossip. C'mon, Earl. Hewitt needs a slug or two. Otherwise he might just as well blow his brains out at that table right now.'

Earl made his decision and handed over the bottle of whiskey to Nevada. Other drinkers had been watching and there was a tense silence as the gunfighter twisted the cork out and set the bottle in front of Hewitt.

In a true drunk's reaction, Hewitt never even looked up, just grabbed the bottle and tilted it against his lips, swigging deeply. He shuddered, started to raise his eyes.

Then the batwings burst open and there was a subdued gasp in the smoky room as Barbara Tate entered, hair wild, eyes roaming the crowd. She soon spotted Nevada and Hewitt and strode across, mouth tightening as she turned a cold gaze on Nevada.

'Damn you! I need him sober! I have an eyewitness to the raiders who burned my line-shack – and what do I find? My own troubleshooter getting the sheriff *drunk*!'

'Not drunk, just fortified. Reckon he's just about right for whatever it is you want him to do. He's picked up his guts – or he's tryin' hard. And I reckon he deserves the chance.'

'Well, I hope so! Because if he does his duty properly, he'll be going up against Calvin Judd!'

CHAPTER 10

DUTY ON THE LINE

It was easy to see why this 'breed they called Jaybird had defected from the mines.

His face was a mess, one cheek laid open by a bullet that looked like it had done its best to tear off his ear as well. The old cloth bandage had slipped down and was black with dried blood, streaks of it showing against the dark skin of his neck. The man was mighty uneasy in the present company: Barbara, Bo Whelan, Sheriff Hewitt and Nevada. It was to Nevada that the dark, shifty eyes kept flicking.

Hewitt had the whiskey bottle with him and turned his back to take a swig. He belched slightly as he swung back. 'Jaybird, I ain't never knowed you to tell the truth yet so why should we b'lieve you now?'

The 'breed shrugged uneasily. 'I dunno. 'Cept what I said is true. Harding gave a bunch of us orders to burn out that line-shack on Bigelow Hill. An' he said no one was to be left alive. It was time them

114

ranchers was taught a lesson.'

'You rode with 'em?' slurred Hewitt, swaying a little but more on the ball than Nevada had expected. Jaybird hesitated and nodded. 'Had to.'

'Sure you did!' scowled Bo Whelan. 'Look, Sheriff, I was ridin' line when this 'breed showed, in the mess you see him now. He said he'd been fired by Harding and they only gave him a few bucks but he figured he had a lot more comin' to him. He said for fifty bucks, he'd tell us what really happened to the line-shack – and who done it.'

Barbara nodded. 'That's correct, Sheriff. Bo brought him in to the ranch and I agreed to pay him his fifty dollars. He said Harding had ordered that raid, and now I want Mr Big-Shot Kyle Harding arrested and jailed.'

Nevada slanted his gaze to her. 'Be right nice for you, huh? With Harding in jail the mine'll likely close, or it'll be some time before a new manager's brought in. Be worth more than fifty bucks, that kind of griff.'

She frowned. 'Don't put expensive ideas into Jaybird's head! We agreed on fifty and we'll stick to it. Right, Jay?'

The 'breed hesitated, obviously thinking now that he had sold out too cheaply, but one look at Bo Whelan and he sighed, nodded. 'We done a deal. I been paid, so I'll be on my way. Don't want to hang around now.'

'You're not goin' anywhere, mister,' Hewitt said, and Nevada was surprised to see the Colt in the sheriff's hand, covering the 'breed. 'You're a material witness. I'm keepin' you locked up till we get Harding behind bars and on his way to court.'

'Oh, no you ain't!' Jaybird said, his voice making his fear of such a thing very plain. 'Judas, they could get to me in a cell, no trouble! Like shootin' a fish in a barrel!'

'You're gonna be locked up, Jay! Bo, you take him on down and lock him in. I gotta get on my way to the mines.'

Whelan grabbed Jaybird's arm and dragged him roughly across the street towards the jailhouse. The 'breed struggled until Bo drew his Colt. They went inside the building.

'Like some back-up?' Nevada asked Hewitt and the sheriff turned quickly.

'No!' he said emphatically. 'This is my chore. I – need this, been needin' somethin' like it for a long time. I can manage alone.' More quietly, he added, 'I got to!'

'Harding won't come easy – and he'll have Judd to back him.'

'I said I'm goin' alone! If I have to, I'll lock you up, too, Nevada.'

The gunfighter nodded slowly. *Hewitt was right – he did need this chore. And if he could pull it off successfully, alone, it would be a big boost for his self-esteem. Might even be able to throw away the bottle eventually. . . .*

With Barbara beside him they watched Hewitt move away towards the livery and, some minutes later, ride out of town without looking back, his rifle across his thighs. The woman's teeth tugged at her lower lip. 'Do you think he can do it?'

'He has to.'

'You think they'll try to kill him?'

'Might. But he's got to do this, find out for himself what kind of a man he's become. . . .'

She seemed about to say something else, then changed her mind and began walking along the boardwalk. Nevada watched the lawman's dwindling figure riding fast now out towards the hills, then started for the livery himself where he had left his mount. Barbara's buggy had been tethered outside the general store. He watched her start for it, then changed his mind and crossed the street, deciding to make sure Bo Whelan hadn't had any trouble with that mean-looking 'breed. The man was vindictive, vengeful, tough, and Nevada wasn't sure anyone could believe his story. But it sounded as if it could be right, although he wondered that Harding would make such an overt raid, which could so easily be traced back to him. . . .

Before he reached the jailhouse, the door opened and Bo Whelan lurched against the frame, sagging, hatless, his nose and mouth bleeding. Nevada sprinted towards him, steadied the man as he tried to haul himself upright.

'The hell happened?'

'God-damned 'breed!' Bo gasped. 'Hit me with the slop bucket, slammed the cell door on me and ran out the back way. I had the keys but couldn't find the right one to open up. Sonuver'll be miles away by now.'

Barbara was driving past in her buggy, saw the drama and hauled rein sharply, standing in the seat.

'Jaybird's run,' Nevada told her. 'Your man's hurt. . . .'

The woman's white face stiffened as she climbed down and confronted the groggy Whelan. 'Couldn't you've stopped him?'

'Caught me off guard.'

Her lip curled contemptuously. 'Obviously! Well, we need that 'breed to nail Harding. You'd better start earning some of that fighting pay, Nevada.'

Bo started to speak as Nevada nodded. 'I'll find him and bring him back.'

That earned him a brief acknowledgement from Barbara. She turned towards Bo, who said: 'It's my chore! I let him get away. Gimme an hour an' I'll run down the son of a bitch before dark.'

'He'll be half-way to Santa Fe or up in Utah by then.' Nevada was already moving away.

'I know this country!' Bo said breathlessly, clinging to the doorframe. He was eager to make amends for his carelessness. What the Tate woman thought of him was obviously important to the ramrod.

'I used to track for the army, Bo – I'll find him.'

'He'll fight!'

'Then I'll shoot him.' The words were flung back over Nevada's shoulder as he hurried back towards the livery.

'He'll do it, Barb! He was an army scout just like he said. He'll find Jaybird all right!'

'Good.'

'I reckon only one of 'em'll walk away.'

Her face didn't change. 'Let's get you patched up.'

118

Kyle Harding was inspecting a pile of treated ore in the special secure hut used for this purpose, Calvin Judd with him, when the sheriff rode in.

'The hell does he want?' gritted Harding, dropping the canvas cover over the dusty box that held the shattered ore with the strong glint of minerals streaking it.

'Can't be much. I'm suprised he could even make the effort to ride this far.'

'My God! He's drunk!' Harding's voice took on a steely edge as Hewitt dismounted and grabbed quickly at his saddle to steady himself as he stumbled.The near-empty whiskey bottle fell to the ground and he made a half-hearted reach for it, but was too dizzy and left it there, hanging on to the saddlehorn by one hand, swaying. 'How the hell did he get a-hold of whiskey?' Harding gritted, rounding on Judd. 'You were supposed to see no one supplied him with it!'

'Damnit! I gave the order. . . .' Judd raised his voice. 'You need a hand there, Sheriff?'

Hewitt made an obvious effort to steady himself and, rifle slanting from his right hand now, slowly and carefully walked towards the men in the entrance to the shed.

'No, I don't need no hand.' His voice was a little slurred and although he seemed loose-limbed and swayed a mite, there was an obvious determination about the lawman. He lifted his left hand, pointing a finger at Kyle Harding. 'You, mister, are unner arrest!'

Harding arched his eyebrows, his face giving no

sign of the alarm he felt suddenly making his heart accelerate. 'That so, Lang? And what am I supposed to've done this time? Pissed in the ranchers' wells? Cut one of their fences? Maybe stole a chicken for my supper? Or have you some other just as stupid and preposterous charge to make on behalf of Barbara Tate and her friends?'

Hewitt stopped, quite steady it seemed now, and swung up the rifle, thumb notching back the hammer.

'Don't get nervous, Judd,' he said as the gunfighter stiffened. 'I already got a shell in the breech and if I have to shoot, you'll be the first target. . . .' He swivelled his red-eyed gaze back to the now frowning Harding. 'How about I charge you with burnin' down the Broken T line-camp on Bigelow Hill? And with the murder of the Westaway boys who died in the fire?'

Harding and Judd were both stunned; it was obvious this was the last thing they had expected. Then Judd spoke quietly: 'Told you we shouldn't've let that damn 'breed go! Would've been easier to pay him what he was owed! Now he's getting his own back, making trouble for us.' He looked soberly at Hewitt. 'That it, Hewitt? Jaybird's your witness?'

'That he is. Locked up where you can't get to him!' Hewitt jerked the rifle barrel slightly. 'Get your hat, Harding – you can have the cell next to Jaybird. And when you saddle him a hoss, Judd, saddle one for yourself, too.'

Judd stiffened even more. 'You're not taking me in!'

Hewitt smiled thinly. 'Harding gave the orders, you carried 'em out. We'll find out later just who rode with you, but you two are the important ones. Now do like I say! I'm takin' you both in and lockin' you up.'

'No!'

Judd snapped the word. An instant later his Colt was blazing as Lang Hewitt was hurled backwards by the strike of lead hammering into his rangy body. He swayed and stumbled, not quite going down, triggered his rifle in a wild shot. Harding yelled and sat down with a thump as Judd put another bullet into the sheriff, spinning him violently.

Hewitt spread out slowly on the ground, still trying to work the lever on his rifle, right up to the moment he drew his last breath.

'You hit bad, Kyle?' Judd asked, reloading as he ran towards Harding who was sitting there, looking at a spreading patch of blood on his shirt-front.

'I'll live. Christ! This is big trouble now you've killed Hewitt! But we can put it partly right by nailing that damn Jaybird! Shut his mouth before he stirs up more trouble! Go and do it!'

Bo Whelan was right: he knew the country better than Nevada and he got to Jaybird first.

Barbara had wanted him to go back to the ranch with her after the doctor tended to his once-again broken nose and split lips, but he said he would stay and have a few drinks: he felt he needed them. She didn't insist, though she drove off a little reluctantly. She knew how vengeful Bo was, and if Nevada brought in Jaybird, the 'breed would have some suffering to do.

But Whelan wasn't about to wait to see the outcome.

He wanted to make the outcome happen.

So, after a couple of redeyes, which stung his lips no end and added to his rising wrath, he got on his horse and quit town at a gallop.

He figured he knew where Jaybird would make for. The 'breed had friends amongst the outcasts who lived back in the hills and Bo had long ago found the secret trails that led to their various hideouts.

He caught up with Jaybird as the man was riding away from one of these, having checked out the big dark caves and found no one there. The 'breed was on his way to the next hiding-place when Whelan settled behind a rock and blew the man out of the saddle with his first shot.

The report of the Winchester slapped and echoed through the hills, dwindling away, as Jaybird rolled heavily. Somehow, he dragged his six-gun free of leather and crawled towards the shelter of some rocks.

'Don't think you're gonna die easy, 'breed! You had your chance and you muffed it by sluggin' me, you son of a. . . .'

Bo's next bullet took Jaybird in the back of the thigh and the 'breed gritted his teeth, trying to strangle the involuntary cry of pain. He twisted on to his back, triggered three fast shots. They were wild but made Bo keep his head down.

When he looked up again, cautiously, Jaybird was

nowhere to be seen. Bo swore, following a blood trail with narrowed eyes, raked the clump of rocks as the lead ricochetted, snarling away into the afternoon. Whelan reloaded, moved to the right through some brush, paused to hammer two more shots at the rocks he knew must be sheltering Jaybird. Chips and dust flew. The sound of gunfire rolled away like distant thunder.

Crouching, Bo waited, then spotted a movement slightly below him between two boulders. It was a narrow gap, too narrow for him to shoot through with success. So, ducking instinctively as Jaybird fired wildly into the brush, nowhere near him, the ramrod moved up-slope, having to grab awkwardly on to a rough-hewn slab of sandstone so as to ease his way around, the only footing on a ledge being but a few inches wide.

If Jaybird spotted him he would make a fine target and he wouldn't even be able to return fire.

But he reached the rock, slid behind it and eased along another three yards. He grinned as he looked over the ledge of broken rock there – looked straight down on the hunched back of the wounded 'breed. There was quite a deal of blood on the ground and the rocks and Bo figured Jaybird was a dead man anyway. He ought to leave him, pretty sure the man would bleed to death in an hour or so; Jaybird would suffer but in the end it would be mostly peaceful, some pain, of course, but then drowsiness would take over, growing heavier and heavier until. . . . That didn't appeal to Bo Whelan.

He had taken that heavy pail across the face and

his throbbing head wouldn't let him forget that in a hurry.

'Hey, 'breed!' he called, chuckling as the man jumped, slipped and sprawled. 'Funny, I thought you always favoured *pink* checked shirts, but that one's mighty red now! Couldn't be your blood makin' it that way, huh?'

The 'breed couldn't see Bo but had his general position from the sound of his voice. He loosed off a shot and the bullet whined away, two yards to the left and way too low. Bo laughed. 'Lousy shot!'

'Bo – I – I din' wanta – hit you,' Jaybird gasped, knowing he was pleading for his life now. 'Couldn't let you – lock me away. . . . Judd woulda found some way to – get to me an' kill me.'

'Forget Judd! *I'm* gonna kill you!'

'Bo – don't! I'm bad hit. Gimme a break! I – I likely won't make it but – lemme try, man! You an' me always got along – OK. Traded a little info over drinks. . . . C'mon! For ol' times' sake. . . . We're on opposite sides now but we used to be – pards, when Ol' Man Tate was alive. . . . We did some hairy jobs for that old bastard together. Gimme a break, huh?'

'Lemme think about it, Jay,' Bo said and almost immediately added, 'Nah! Can't do it! You never could be trusted! So long, you half-breed son of a bitch!'

Jaybird had him spotted just as Bo raised up to put the killing shot into the man. They fired together and Bo Whelan was astonished as rock chips raked his face and a large piece of sandstone smacked him in the middle of the forehead, drawing fresh blood and knocking him sideways.

Dazed, bright lights flashing before his eyes, he dragged himself back to the ledge and warily looked over. He managed a crooked smile through the pain in his head.

Jaybird was sprawled face down, unmoving, a spreading patch of red between his shoulders.

Bo sat up, reaching for a kerchief to mop his face. He looked around, casually, but alert to anyone coming who might have been attracted by all the shooting. His gaze went to the next range of hills, mistily visible across a large, deep draw.

'Well, now. . . ! I don't believe it! I get to square me away two grudges on the same day!'

Nevada Hawk was easing his mount slowly down the slope, weaving a cautious trail, heading in this direction.

Bo smiled thinly and began to reload his rifle before settling back to wait.

CHAPTER 11

GUNSMOKE

Calvin Judd hadn't yet decided how he was going to silence the traitorous Jaybird.

There was no question that the man had to be silenced, but should he walk right in to the jailhouse and shoot the 'breed through the bars, or should he be a bit more subtle, find himself a rooftop where he could see into the cellblock and pick Jaybird off with his rifle?

It was a pleasant quandary, the kind Judd enjoyed mulling over, for he was a man who liked to see blood – as long as it belonged to someone else.

As he entered Main he had a sort of itch which was bothering him, but it was not specific enough for him to scratch – unless it was his head under his brown hat. But, no: it was a feeling he had experienced before several times. It was actually a hunch, warning him to be careful, that things weren't just the way they seemed.

126

So he dismounted in front of the jailhouse, looped his reins over the hickory crossbar and hitched at his gunbelt before entering.

The local part-time deputy whom Hewitt employed now and again was snoring in a chair behind the low rail that separated the office from the entry area. Judd scowled and then turned to the door that led into the cellblock, went in and down the dim passage,Colt in hand – and found all cells empty. The knot in his belly began to unravel and the itch went away; this was what his hunch was trying to tell him!

The luckless deputy awoke with a start and a wild-eyed look. He thumped heavily to the floor after Judd deliberately tilted the man's chair well past the point of balance. He was a gangling man with a big Adam's apple, slow to anger – in fact, slow to do anything – and he frowned at Judd as he staggered upright.

'Where's the 'breed?' the gunfighter demanded, his words causing the deputy to frown more deeply and screw up his face.

'Don't hev no 'breed here.'

'Goddamnit, I know that! He's supposed to be in one of the cells. Now where is he?'

The deputy shook his head slowly, dusted off his old wrinkled clothes, then reached down to pick up the overturned chair. Judd swore softly, stepped forward and kicked the chair from the man's grasp, fisted-up his shirt front and bent him back over the desk, ignoring papers and writing-sets that spilled and clattered to the floor.

'Hey! you cain't. . . !' The deputy stopped, swallowed as Judd's gun barrel pressed under his lantern jaw, forcing his head back. 'Easy there! I – I'm a duly-sworn deputy, 'case you dunno—'

'You'll be a sick-and-sorry deputy in about one minute flat if you don't tell me *where the hell that 'breed, Jaybird, is!*'

The pressure of the blade foresight under his jawbone made the man whimper and his eyes widened even more. 'I – dunno. He slugged Bo Whelan an' nobody knows where he went.'

Judd paused, stiffening a little. 'He – busted out?' The deputy nodded vigorously but Judd still held him with his back arched across the desk and the gun barrel under his jaw. 'Who went after him . . . ?'

'No one far as I know. Lang Hewitt had already gone to the mine to arrest Kyle Harding an' . . . you, too! What you doin' here? Where's Lang. . . ?'

Judd eased his grip, hauled the man upright and sighed. 'The sheriff's . . . discussing things with Mr Harding. Jaybird told a pack of lies. You any idea where that 'breed'd go?'

The deputy shrugged then, sniffing, at last beginning to feel put-upon, said: 'He used to hang out in the hills with Kernigan's wild bunch. Far as I know they's still there – But, listen, Mr Judd, you cain't come in here and rough me up like I'm no one! I'm a—'

'Yeah, yeah, I know – you're a duly-sworn deputy. I'm sorry. I was so riled about the lies that 'breed told about me and Mr Harding. . . .' He patted the deputy's shoulder, produced a silver dollar and slipped it into the man's wrinkled shirt-pocket. 'Go have yourself a drink, friend. I've got some riding to do.'

'Oh. Thanks, Mr Judd. Hey . . . you know when the sheriff'll be back?'

Judd paused in the doorway. 'I wouldn't look for him for some time yet.'

'Holy hell! Am I. . . I s'posed to watch this place all night?'

'No one in the cells. I was you, I'd lock up, go have my drink and then head for home.'

The deputy had to give that some thought, but by the time he'd done that Judd was on the move.

That damn Jaybird! He had to be stopped – and stopped dead.

He looked beyond town at the misty mountains and the mesa. If Jaybird was in there it would take a year to find him – but he had to be found and right quick!

He mounted and rode fast out of town in the mellowing afternoon light. Judd disliked the discomfort of camping out, but that was what he would have to do this night.

And maybe many more nights to come.

Bo Whelan was not only impatient, but uneasy now.

Where the hell was Nevada?

The man had entered deep into the draw long ago and although the tops of the trees had hidden him there should have been some sign of him by now. There was an outcrop of ancient brown, lichen-scabbed rocks that could have hidden his crossing to the base of the slope, but he should be moving up towards where Bo waited by now.

He eased up slowly, looking between two boulders in front of him. His head was throbbing and his eyes weren't as sharp as they should be, but they would be good enough to see so he could shoot Nevada out of the saddle. Jaybird could take the blame.

He had moved higher, into the better protection of larger rocks, and he was now unable to see Jaybird's body below. His plan was for Nevada to spot the dead 'breed, ride in and dismount to examine the body. He would see him doing that. Then Bo would put a bullet into him – not a fatal one: no sir, that would be too easy for this son of a bitch! He would call out, taunt the drifter while he squirmed in agony, and then take his time about finishing the man off. Bullet-bust his limbs, one by one, maybe get one into his belly, let him roll and plead for the finishing shot before he finally blew the man's brains out.

'You'll know before you die, that no one makes a damn fool outta Bo Whelan and gets away with it!' he growled half-aloud for perhaps the tenth time since first sighting Nevada.

'Aw, I dunno,' said a voice behind Bo that brought a crop of goosebumps out on his flesh that felt as big as quail's eggs. 'I'm not doing too bad. I've just fooled you again.'

Bo spun around, bringing his rifle with him, firing way too soon, but hoping the explosion would distract Nevada.

But Nevada didn't move. He was standing in front of one of the larger boulders, rifle in both hands, pointed at the now rolling Bo. Nevada shot him through the right leg and Bo screamed, grabbing at the wound with his left hand as blood oozed between the spread fingers.

'*Jeee-sussss!*' he gritted, then brought the rifle over, trying to lever a shell into the breech with his blood-slippery fingers. Nevada shook his head slowly, working the lever of his own rifle.

'Don't think you can do it before I nail you, Bo.'

Bo, breathing hard, let the rifle sag, tore the bandanna from around his neck and twisted it before wrapping it tightly above the bleeding wound in his leg. He held it so it put pressure on the wound. 'I'm gonna – bleed to death!'

'Yeah, there's a pretty good chance of that. You didn't give Jaybird much of a chance, though, did you?'

Whelan snapped his head up, frowning slightly at Nevada's tone. 'He – spotted me, tried to bushwhack me – was him or me.'

'Well, you had to make sure he was dead, I can see that. But he said you were the one set the ambush.'

The ramrod stiffened. 'He *said?* He's been dead an hour!' There was a coldness in his belly now as Nevada shook his head slowly.

'No. He's dead now. But we had us a little talk before he finally cashed in. You're too far back from the edge of that drop or you'd likely have seen me find him. I came round the draw. It looked like an old riverbed to me and I was checking it out when I came across Jaybird. You hit him bad, but he was hanging on, wanted to tell what was bothering him before he died.'

Bo stared. 'You're a liar!'

Nevada shrugged. 'You mean Jaybird lied, with his last few minutes of breath? Not likely, Bo. He said that after he quit Harding he looked you up for a handout; seems you knew each other from way back and Harding had done him wrong, wouldn't pay what he figured he was owed. So you made a deal with Jay, said if he told Barbara and anyone else who'd listen, that it was Judd led the attack on the line-camp, on Harding's orders, you'd see Barbara paid him enough so he could get clear of this neck of the woods—'

'Why the hell would I do that? I don't make deals with 'breeds. Not even ones I know from way back when.'

'Well, you made a deal with Jaybird – not for old times' sake, but because you had no choice: because he'd seen you lead some men in to attack and burn the line-camp.'

Bo narrowed his pain-filled eyes and said scathingly: 'Hogwash! Why in the hell would I do a stupid, lousy thing like that?'

'Maybe because Barbara told you to?'

'What! You plumb loco? Her own line-camp. . . ? Judas priest, the Westaways were in there. . . !'

Nevada nodded slowly. 'They were, Bo. And that's why I'm going to kill you. The Westaways might've been a bit different, but they weren't doing anyone any harm – they kept to themselves, just kids. *OK* kids, at that. And you burned 'em to death, then did your best to do the same to me in the storehouse.'

Bo was sweating profusely now. Some was from the pain as it took hold, running in electric snakes from the wound right through his body and up into his brain, making him gasp, his chest heaving. The rest was from cold fear.

He shook his head rapidly, but it made him even more dizzy and he stopped, blinking. 'You – can't believe no 'breed!'

'A dying man – 'breed, black, brindle or white – don't waste breath making up lies, Bo. He's got something on his mind, he makes sure it gets said before he cashes in.'

Bo had nowhere to go – literally – and he knew it. His nostrils were pinched white now. 'You can't prove any of that.'

'Maybe I'm a man who don't need proof with every "i" dotted and each "t" crossed, Bo. I can see how it could be the way Jaybird told it.'

'Look! You . . . you're a johnny-come-lately! You dunno diddly-squat about this valley! I been workin' for Broken T for nigh on fifteen years! Came as a shaver and old man Tate took a shine to me, treated me right. I'd do anythin' to see the spread stays the way he wanted it, and that includes lookin' out for Barbara.'

'She strikes me as a woman who's quite able to look after herself, but I guess having a snake like you as a sidekick might help things along at times – and if she didn't have much of a conscience. Or if there were things going on she didn't know about. So maybe it *was* all your idea to hit the line-camp and burn it, kill those two kids. Why? To get the whole valley up in arms against the mines, even pull Lang Hewitt on side – and *he'd* have sent for a US marshal for back-up. He'd have to, being what he is. And that means Broken T and the other spreads would have federal law backing. All for the cost of a couple of lives and a line-shack that could be rebuilt in a few weeks. Killing me at the same time would've been mighty convenient, too, eh, Bo?'

Bo was silent now except for his laboured breathing, He rubbed at the bloody trouser-leg, watching Nevada's face. 'You dunno what you're talkin' about – but you could cause a lot of trouble, bandyin' them things about. . . .' Bo looked shrewd through the pain. 'Not that you'd have to talk about 'em.'

'No, I wouldn't . . . *have* to.'

A glimmer of hope showed on Bo's gaunt face. 'Barb's got a slew of cash stashed away at the house. Name a price and I'll see if I can negotiate a deal for you. You could leave here a rich man, Nevada.'

'You'd do that for me? The man who made you look a fool in front of your cowhands?'

Bo shrugged. 'We-ell. Circumstances, you know. . . .'

He shrugged, grimaced as he moved his lower body, looking beaten and like a man in great pain. He was both those things, but then his six-gun whipped up and he fired twice across his body.

Nevada's rifle blasted simultaneously, even as he staggered from the strike of Bo's bullet.

Bo Whelan slammed over violently, the high impact of the rifle bullet rolling him completely over on to his shattered face. The Colt flew from his grip, his legs jerked and twitched for a few seconds before he slumped and seemed to collapse in on himself and become a part of the blood-soaked earth on the slope.

Nevada levered a fresh shell into the breech before laying the rifle down within reach. He lifted the torn and bloody shirt away from his left shoulder, found that Bo Whelan's slug had burned across the muscle running from neck to shoulder, gouging away a chunk of flesh, but missing the collar-bone and anything else of a serious nature.

He wadded his neckerchief and stuffed it over the bleeding wound, buttoned the shirt-collar firmly so it would hold the cloth in place.

Then he leaned back against the rock, took out his tobacco sack and papers and slowly built a cigarette.

There were two dead men within a few yards of him. He had to do something about them and then, he guessed, he had better go find out how Lang Hewitt had got on with his confrontation with Kyle Harding.

And Calvin Judd.

CHAPTER 12

MOVING MOUNTAINS

Nevada had never left a dead man for the wild animals. If he came across one on the trail he buried it somehow, at least covered it with rocks. He had seen what wild animals did to corpses left in the open and figured any man deserved a better end than that.

So, even though his wounded shoulder hurt and started bleeding more profusely, he got Bo Whelan draped over the man's horse and worked his way down-slope to where he had left Jaybird after the man had died in his arms amongst the rocks.

Most of the rocks here were larger than he could lift and set firmly in the ground, anyway. But he remembered passing an overhanging ledge that he had skirted because it did not look very safe. It was a hundred yards away but he got both bodies over there, laid them underneath, then cut a sapling. He stood to one side, poking and gouging at the under-side, then moved to the other and did the same thing. It was nearly dark before the cutbank collapsed and a ton of earth spilled over the dead men.

Nevada fell sprawling as he ran to get out of the way, landed on his left side and jarred the shoulder. The pain was bad and he felt as though his arm was being torn off. He sat there for a few minutes, hold-ing the shoulder, letting the dust settle around him. He washed the wound with canteen water, tore up an old shirt in his war bag and devised a crude sling. His arm felt better resting in the sling but the reposi-tioning made him feel slightly off balance.

This slope was too steep for a campsite and the darkness was closing in. He didn't want to go down all the way into the draw, for he would only have to climb back in the morning to get over this part of the mountain, so as to find the trail to the Amarosa mine. Or, if his wound acted up, he might have to abandon that idea and head back for the Broken T.

He had no wish to square off with a man as fast with a gun as Calvin Judd when his arm might throw his balance at the crucial moment.

He went to the loose earth at the edge of the mound formed by the collapsing cutbank and began to dig a shallow hole in which to bury his bloody bandages. As he was doing it, in the last rays of the setting sun, he saw something glinting, small but bright. Curious, he picked it up, thinking it was a spent bullet. It wasn't.

It was a small nugget of gold.

*

Calvin Judd didn't feel easy being out in the hills just on sundown. He was essentially a townsman, liked a solid roof between him and the stars at night, good strong walls surrounding him and, when necessary, a fire in the grate.

And because he wasn't an outdoor man he got himself lost in the hills when darkness closed down. He swore, viciously, to help cover the tightening in his belly and the bile in his throat that told him his usual nervousness at the thought of spending the night alone out here was waiting in the shadows, ready to pounce upon him. *Like the unseen wild animals he had feared since childhood.*

There were beads of sweat on his face and, irritably, he mopped them away with a kerchief. *By God, if anyone ever found out how being alone in the dark of the hills affected him. . . ! He would be a laughing-stock!*

That thought, strangely, gave him the strength to overcome the fear. *Yes! He had to admit it to himself: he was afraid out here – like a damn kid!*

But he knew enough to find himself a safe place and searched in the fading light for a small cave. He located one and warily checked it out for habitation, with six-gun at the ready. There was animal spoor but it was very old and he felt comfortable enough with that. He gathered brush for a bed, made a small fire and brewed coffee, chewing on jerky which he hated, thinking of the gourmet meals he had shared with Harding in the man's luxurious quarters back at the Amarosa.

He went outside to relieve himself before turning in and was buttoning up, looking around casually, when he suddenly froze.

Higher up the slope, on a ledge he had seen before making camp, there was the glow of another camp-fire, a little bigger than his own.

Jaybird? he wondered.

The one thing he hated more than camping out at night was travelling through the dark. So it took no real effort to convince himself that not even a dimwit like the 'breed, on the run, would make a fire out where it would give away his position. He retired to his brush bed, but sleep wouldn't come. He had to check out that damn fire. If it wasn't Jaybird, maybe it was that mysterious rider who had been seen in the hills and on the outlying ranch land. Harding wanted to know who he was and what he was doing.

Cursing, he rolled out of his bed and groped for his hat and boots.

Nevada felt the heat of the camp-fire wash over him as he stood at the edge of the brush, rifle held down at his side but with a cartridge in the breech and his thumb on the hammer spur.

He stood motionless, only his eyes moving as he looked around the camp. There were two burros picketed near some brush which they were devouring, ears flicking, eyes rolling, but that was the only interest they showed in him. There was a dust-caked horse a little way along, ground-hitched on some grass. Between the mount and burros was tumbled gear: wooden frames, a riffle-board, a disassembled rocker-cradle, and some rust-flecked gold-panning dishes.

This looked like the camp of a prospector, Nevada allowed silently, but where was he?

'Just come on in easy, feller!' a gravelly voice ordered him from the deep shadows of the trees opposite where Nevada was standing. Nevada held the rifle out from his side, letting the hidden man see his arm in the sling. 'Saw your fire from down below. . . .'

It was some time before the man answered, night-birds and insects filling in the gap with their noise. 'Step closer to the fire.'

Nevada obeyed and waited while the hidden man looked him over. 'I'll lay my rifle on the ground if you want.'

'Yeah, do that and step back.'

Nevada obeyed, his right hand lifted shoulder-high now, eyes narrowing against the glare of the fire as the man stepped out. He was medium height, broad-shouldered, and his shirt sleeves rolled to the elbows showed tanned, muscular forearms. There was stubble on a narrow, tanned, fairly pleasant face, lined deeply by many years of weather. Nevada figured the man was about forty. His trousers were tucked into the tops of dusty, scuffed leather half-boots. The only weapon he carried, that Nevada could see, anyway, was the Winchester carbine, now trained on the drifter.

'You'd be. . . ?'

'Folks call me Nevada.'

The man nodded. 'Figured so. Been hearin' about

you. Killed some men, didn't you?' Nevada said nothing and a half-smile lifted the man's mouth. 'My name's Stoddart – Lacy Stoddart.'

'Kin to the rancher down in the valley?'

Stoddart nodded. 'Brother. Not that me an' Matt see much of each other.'

Nevada studied the man a little, then said, quietly: 'Not when you're off prospecting, I guess. Matt send for you?'

Lacy Stoddart frowned, his gaze sharpening a little. 'I heard you weren't dumb, but what made you ask that?'

'Just don't get an itchy trigger finger. Want to show you something.' Nevada worked the small gold nugget out of his shirt-pocket and held it out in the palm of his hand. Firelight glinted on the yellow metal. 'Found it downslope. Wondered how much more there might be.'

Stoddart continued to size up Nevada, then lowered the carbine's hammer and walked to the deadfall beside the fire. 'Have some java and we'll talk.'

Nevada, relieved that the man wasn't going to shoot him, relaxed and eased his arm in the sling. At Stoddart's querying look he told him about Bo Whelan.

'Well, that son of a bitch ain't gonna be missed. Good cowman, by all counts, but a mite short on what makes a decent man. I seen you a couple times when I was lookin' around. You din' see me, though.'

Nevada smiled. 'Wrong. I spotted you twice, thought you were either one of Barbara Tate's crew I hadn't met or something to do with Harding and the

Amarosa. You were too far away to hail.'

Lacy Stoddart chuckled. 'Yeah, well, guess I'm gettin' a little too easy-goin' these days. Should've checked you out better.'

'You find much gold?' The prospector drank from his mug and didn't reply. 'Had a hunch there might be some minerals in the ranch land and that's why Harding was poisoning the water supply – didn't know there was enough gold in this neck of the woods to prospect with an outfit like you've got. I'd say this isn't your first time.'

'First up here. But, you're right. There ain't much of the yaller stuff around. That nugget you found and half a dozen more I came up with is the result of two months' prospectin'. Oh, yeah, you could say there's gold here, all right. There is. Maybe some small pockets but mostly scattered to hell an' gone. It ain't paydirt.'

Nevada frowned. 'Then why would Harding be interested? I'm pretty sure there's something more behind the water pollution than just the mine company being too lazy or too cheap to build proper run-off drains.'

Stoddart smiled, nodded thanks as Nevada passed over his tobacco sack and papers. 'I said not much paydirt. I meant for a loner like me to make it worth while workin', or even a half-dozen men. Too little for that. But for a big mine, with their methods and machines, they could likely make it worth while: dig a hole half-way to China, process the dirt, recover all the little bits of gold – and watch the pile grow while they process the other minerals, too. They could

142

even strike a reef. Be mighty deep, though.'

Nevada took a burning twig from the fire and lit both cigarettes. 'So, move the mountains and grow rich. Try to grub it away a little at a time and all you'd do is wear out your tools – and yourself.'

'That's the way it appears. Matt asked me to come up and check. Like you, he had a notion there might be gold on his land and that's why Harding was being so hard-nosed about pollutin' his creek, tryin' to drive him out. My guess is the copper an' zinc are runnin' low and the Amarosa Company don't want to shut down a mine they've spent a small fortune settin' up. So, they're lookin' around and if they can find gold. . . .' He shrugged.

'How did Harding know about the gold?'

Stoddart shrugged. 'Likely hired someone to look around on the quiet, got a report back to say there was gold found but could be a big operation to get at it. Might not even've mentioned that part. Harding knows the ranches would never sell at the price he'd offer so he decided to drive 'em out by runnin' his waste into their creeks. That's my guess, anyway.'

'He made some feeble efforts to correct that run-off. I took a look at the elevated sluiceway and it's in the wrong place, far too close to the creek.'

'Meant to be. But Amarosa can still claim they tried their best to take the waste away from the ranches' water supply. That'd keep the law out of it and, on paper, on their side.'

'Harding must have worried when the law was in the shape of Lang Hewitt, a drunk, liable to swing any way that suited him, as long as there was easy booze on offer. They must have thrown a blue fit when Hewitt decided it was time he made an effort to live up to his oath of office . . . By God!' he said suddenly, spilling his coffee and startling Stoddart. 'They'd kill him if he tried to pull rank on 'em!'

'The hell goosed you all of a sudden?' Stoddart was still startled.

'The sheriff went to Amarosa to arrest Harding for raiding a Broken T line-camp.'

'That weren't Harding! I saw part of that raid. Bo Whelan and a couple of hardcases ridin' away, the place blazin'. Wondered why he burned his own line-camp. See it now. Tryin' to get the law on the side of Broken T by blamin' it on Amarosa.'

'That's it, I—'

'And it all went wrong.'

Both men whirled. Nevada dropped a hand to his gunbutt but lost his balance because of his sling-immobilized left arm. By the time he straightened, he was covered by Calvin Judd's six-gun as the man stepped into the camp.

He looked closely at Stoddart but didn't ignore Nevada either as the man straightened, keeping his hand away from his Colt now. 'So, you're the mystery rider the men've been telling us about. Thought you were some government snooper seeing how bad the creek was polluted by the mine's run-off.'

'Lacy Stoddart, brother to Matt. Just doin' him a favour,' the prospector explained, sounding unafraid.

Judd curled a lip, much more confident now that he was in the camp with the upper hand. 'Snooping!

Checking out the gold content! Yes, I heard you telling Nevada all about it. Puts me in something of a quandary.'

Stoddart frowned. 'How's that?'

'Well, we don't want you spreading it around about the gold and how it's unprofitable for a lone prospector to work, but perfectly viable for a mining company like Amarosa with their machinery and refining methods.'

The look on Stoddart's face told Nevada the prospector saw that, clearly enough.

'What's the problem then?' he asked and Judd smiled thinly as he turned his gaze to the drifter.

'You don't count, Nevada, you're dead anyway. By rights you both should die, but I think we need Stoddart alive. He's an independent witness that Whelan raided and burned and murdered those two Westaway kids and so Amarosa's off the hook. Which means me and Kyle.'

Nevada could see that but his voice was tight as he asked: 'Did Hewitt arrest Harding yet?'

Judd chuckled, shaking his head. 'He won't be arresting anybody!'

Nevada stiffened, eyes narrowing. 'I suppose you prodded Hewitt into going for his gun.'

Judd smiled. 'I won't be notching my gunbutt. Not worthy of remembering, gunning down the town drunk! My God, I wouldn't want that on my record!'

'Maybe it won't bother you one way or t'other,' suggested Nevada quietly and his words brought a slight frown to Judd's face.

'It'd bother me all right.'

'Not if you're dead.'

It was just enough to startle Judd, enough for the man to realize that Nevada wasn't making an idle threat. He froze for an instant. And in that instant, Nevada's Colt came up blasting. Although Judd was astonishingly fast in his recovery, Nevada's bullet struck him a split second before he fired.

Judd's slug took Nevada's hat off and sent it spinning. The drifter moved fast, his wounded shoulder ramming into the blinking prospector, knocking him over the deadfall where the man instinctively crawled in close and hugged the ground. Judd was twisting away, doubling up with the searing pain of Nevada's lead across his lower ribs on the right side. The impact flung his gun arm outwards and his second shot missed the drifter, too.

Nevada dived over the deadfall, several feet from where Stoddart lay huddled. Lead flung splinters into his face as he hit, rolled, and scrabbled swiftly back against the log. His head was ringing and his neck was on fire, the shoulder wound bleeding and hammering him with pain.

Judd was beside himself with rage: he had had Nevada cold, dead to rights! And the man had still out-smarted him – he knew it really came down to *outdrawn* him but he couldn't allow himself to admit that. But it had to be put right! And that meant Nevada had to die – or Judd did.

As the thought crashed into his brain, he ran forward, shooting at the small part of Nevada's body that was visible. Splinters thrummed from the log and Nevada wrenched around, rose to one knee, his

146

hand chopping at the hammer spur.

Judd's mad charge had carried him almost up to the log and he stopped in his tracks as Nevada appeared before him, Colt blazing.

Calvin Judd died where he stood, folded like a collapsing cardboard cut-out, jerking and shuddering, and draped himself over the splintered deadfall.

Nevada was already automatically reloading his smoking six-gun when Lacy Stoddart breathed, awestruck, as he stood shakily: 'Judas *priest!*'

CHAPTER 13

ONE MAN'S FUTURE

Nevada had never met Matt Stoddart although he knew the man was supposed to be an ally of Barbara Tate's.

But he rode to the Stoddart ranch – it was closer than Broken T – with Lacy Stoddart and his burros, and the body of Calvin Judd draped over the gunfighter's own horse under a blanket.

Matt Stoddart was an older version of Lacy, somewhere in his late forties, maybe early fifties, was Nevada's guess. He screwed his gaze into Nevada as Lacy explained, with some excitement, about what had happened out in the hills.

'So you're as good with a gun as they say?' Matt remarked when his brother had finished. 'And your fists, too, I guess, if what I hear about you and Bo Whelan is true.'

148

Nevada silently turned his face so the rancher could see the fading bruises and cuts. Matt smiled thinly.

'Uh-huh. I could use a man like you.'

Nevada hesitated. 'Think I'm still working for Broken T.'

'You'll go on workin' for Barbara? Even if she ordered Whelan to burn that line-camp? With the two young daisies inside?'

'I haven't asked her about that yet.'

'Goin' to?'

'I'll get 'round to it. Right now, we need to figure the next move.'

Matt poured a round of stiff drinks and they sipped the whiskey after raising the glasses in a silent toast. The rancher smacked his lips, glanced at his brother.

'What you figure, Lacy? This is all Harding's doing? Or did he have orders from Amarosa?'

The prospector frowned into his glass. 'I've come across 'em before, in other territories. They're tough and they're in the game to make a profit, but I never heard of 'em deliberately breakin' the law or gettin' anyone killed because they were in their way. They seem to figure everyone has a price. So I'd say this was Harding's notion. For some reason he had a hunch there was gold scattered about and figured to do himself some good with the mining company by gettin' them the lease, even if the land was bein' ranched.'

'If he's been in the mining game for a long time – and I suspect he has,' Nevada said, 'he might've got the notion from that draw between the hills. It's an old river course and it could've scattered alluvial gold for miles before it dried up. Over the years, floods would spread the gold around even more.'

'Well, however he got the idea, he played his hunch and we've been the ones to suffer,' Matt Stoddart said, grim-faced. 'I've lost more stock than Broken T and if it keeps on, I'll lose a lot more . . . eventually, the whole damn ranch!'

'And Harding'll move in with a low offer which you won't have no choice but to accept,' the rancher's brother said. 'With what we've got, I figure we could get the law in to move on our behalf, Matt. But Nevada here found out that Judd killed Lang Hewitt. So where's that leave you?'

Matt shrugged, baring his teeth as he poured another drink for everyone. 'Danglin'! I'll have to see a lawyer, get all the facts, send for a US marshal. Only thing is, by that time, I'll have a big hole in my herds that I'll never plug before round-up and trailin' season. Broken T'll be the same and the smaller ranches'll be wiped out long before us.'

'There's another way.' The brothers looked sharply towards Nevada as he spoke. 'We get all the ranchers to pool their crews and we ride in on the Amarosa.'

There was a silence in the big old ranch living-room with the smoke-stained walls and rafters.

'You tryin' to start an all-out war?' demanded Matt crankily. 'Man, we've been tryin' to avoid that for months!'

'And men have died during that time, Matt. I'm

no animal-hater but I'd put a man's life before that of a prime steer any day.'

'He's right, Matt,' Lacy Stoddart said quietly.

Tight-lipped, Matt nodded slowly. 'He may be. But Harding employs a lot more hardcases than just Calvin Judd. He has 'em on stand-by, payin' 'em fightin' wages. We ride in there and we'll be dodgin' flying lead ten seconds later.'

'There's still a way of doing it,' Nevada insisted. Although Matt was reluctant, he agreed to listen to the drifter's plan.

Kyle Harding knew that something must've happened to Judd. It wasn't like the man to stay out in the wilderness all this time. He would have found some excuse to come back long before this.

Some of his men had reported hearing gunfire in the hills on a few separate occasions and Harding feared the worst. Already he was checking through his list of hardcases, trying to find a replacement for Judd, should the worst have happened: and he knew damn well, deep down, that it *had!*

There was one man, a big, good-looking *hombre* named Rocco, who favoured sideburns, and Harding had to admit that their jet-black colour went well with his swarthy skin. But to hell with the way he looked. Rocco was still a killer and a cold son of a bitch. More than once Judd had had to restrain him. He had beaten one of the smaller ranches' cowhands to death and they had been lucky to cover it up as an accident, running the man's horse over a cliff and dumping the body after it on to a field of rocks.

Not that Rocco wasn't intelligent: it was just that he was hard to control. And Harding's problem now was that he wasn't certain *he* could control the big man now that Judd wasn't here. *Oh, Christ! Let me be wrong about that! Let Judd come riding in here right now – alive and thirsting for blood as usual! That's the way I really want it. . . .*

His prayer wasn't exactly answered: Calvin Judd did return to the Amarosa mine quite soon, but he was roped over his horse with a bloodstained blanket draped over his body.

Sweating, and with stomach knotting, as soon as the news was brought to him Kyle Harding appeared on the porch of his living-quarters, pulling on his frock-coat to hide his shoulder holster. He narrowed his gaze. Nevada was sitting his horse at his ease beside the other animal which carried Judd's body.

'What d'you want, Nevada?' Harding said in a steady voice; he wasn't quite sure how he managed it, but somehow he did. 'If that's Calvin Judd's body—'

'It is. Got four of my bullets in him.'

Harding smiled crookedly and looked around at the men now gathering. He found Rocco adjusting his hat carefully on his black hair so he wouldn't disturb it too much: he was a vain man. Harding locked gazes with Rocco and nodded gently: he knew the man would understand. Judd was dead; the top gunslinger's job was now his.

Rocco smiled and strutted forward, squaring already square shoulders, hooking his thumbs arrogantly in his gunbelt as he looked up at Nevada. 'Mister, you've got yourself a passel of trouble.'

'Not from you.'

Rocco's cocky smile vanished and he stiffened. But Harding, a little afraid of the man's hair-trigger temper, stepped in smartly.

'Rocco means if you killed Judd, you'll have some explaining to do, Nevada.'

'Fair and square. He tried to kill me but he wasn't good enough.' Nevada paused, added: 'I have a witness, too.'

'One of your rancher cronies?'

'No. Independent witness. A man who didn't even know Judd, barely knows me. He saw it all. And he's a man of good standing, Harding. A prospector and mineralogist. . . .'

Nevada watched the sudden uncertainty on Harding's face change to fear as the words sank in. 'So. . . ?'

'So, he'll swear it was a fair shoot-out, and he'll also swear to what he found while prospecting the riverbottoms – and that'll set a lot of folk wondering about how come your mine is still poisoning the cattle and feed of the ranchers who work that land. Could it be to ruin them so the mine can move in and take over, working the land for gold and making it a paying proposition?'

There was silence in the yard, except for the distant, unending thump of the stamp-mill and crusher on the far side of the hill. Rocco's head snapped around.

'Gold? Here?'

Harding held up a hand but swiftly lowered it when he realized how badly it was shaking. 'I think

153

that, perhaps, Nevada, it would be best if you kept such wild accusations to yourself.' He turned to Rocco and nodded. 'There's really only one way to ensure that, so – *Rocco! Earn your pay!*'

Rocco's hand blurred to his gun but Nevada had already rammed home his spurs and his horse, whinnying in fright, leapt forward its full length. It smashed into the hardcase and sent him spilling to the ground. Rocco, dazed, rolled wildly to get out of the way of the hoofs, and Nevada leaned casually out of the saddle and gunwhipped the man as he surged up, face twisted with a lust to kill.

Rocco staggered and Nevada's gun barrel cracked again on the man's skull, knocking his hat flying this time. Rocco stretched out, blood oozing down from his hairline, across his now grey but still handsome face.

Nevada wheeled the mount and fired two shots at the feet of the line of Harding's hardcases as they belatedly reached for their weapons.

'Don't try it, boys!' Nevada stood in the stirrups and pointed with his stiff and sore wounded arm, unable to lift it very high without wincing.

There was a line of horsemen in a giant horseshoe along the ridge of the slope. All had rifles or shotguns and the hardcases slowly lifted their hands, not meeting Harding's panic-stricken gaze. With a whining cry he snatched at the hand-made Remington Guardian model revolver he carried in the shoulder holster under his jacket.

Nevada shot him through the hand as the gun appeared and Harding screamed, dropped the pistol, clapped his shattered hand against his chest. He fell to his knees, bending over in pain as the cattlemen moved in.

'This mine's shutting down for a spell, gents,' Nevada said to the mine workers who watched apprehensively. 'A US marshal will be along in due course to sort things out. But I think Harding will be in jail for a long time, and maybe some of you with him.' He addressed this last to the tight bunch of the worried-looking hardcases. 'Unless you'd like to take the chance I'm giving you to hightail it out of here and never come back. You workmen stay put. You'll have your jobs to do again pretty soon. . . .'

He didn't have to say any more. Already the hardcases had broken lines and were running for their mounts.

Nevada had his arm back in a sling. But this time it was a proper sling, arranged and adjusted by the local doctor and his nurse wife. This was the fifth day now and the sawbones had pronounced the wound well on the way to healing.

'Lucky it wasn't my gun arm, I guess,' Nevada said. 'I'm gonna have to ask you to trust me for payment, Doc—'

The sawbones held up his hand. 'All taken care of – Barbara Tate.'

Now, standing on the boardwalk outside the Wells Fargo depot, Nevada looked down into Barbara's face as she pushed her hat back and allowed some curls to twist across her forehead. She was dressed in her shirt and trousers as usual, looked a little drawn, but she smiled at the drifter.

'I wish you'd stay on, Nevada. We owe you plenty. Amarosa is sending down one of their bigwigs to sort things out and he says in his wire that they intend to prosecute Harding, even if the law doesn't find something to charge him with.'

'They'll find something without much effort after what he tried to pull. But it's time I moved along. I came here to kill the man who murdered my wife and I've done that. Reckon I'll be better off putting a lot of miles between Castle Rock and me. I've enough memories to carry around without seeing this place every day.'

She studied his face. 'You – you're still not – certain sure I didn't condone Bo Whelan's raiding the line-camp in an effort to have Harding blamed, are you?'

He looked down into her face, his own unreadable. As it happened he *wasn't* sure she hadn't gone along with Whelan. Maybe she hadn't put him up to it but maybe – just maybe – after Bo had done it, she couldn't resist the chance to use it to nail Harding by blaming him and his hardcases. *She was an opportunist. Look how she'd used him. . . .*

She sighed, shaking her head. 'Well, as I said, thanks to you, we've got a chance now. They're going to divert the mine run-off through that old watercourse, like it should've been in the first place. The clean river will bring plenty of water to our ranches and all along the bottomland. By the way, I owe you some money.'

She held out some folded paper money and he took it without counting it, placed it in his shirt-pocket. It would get him out of here and that was what counted now. He had no love for this place.

Then the stage rolled in and amid the billowing dust of its arrival the passengers alighted. Barbara looked steadily into his face and then smiled suddenly and held out her hand. He shook briefly.

'I – actually wanted to kiss you . . .' she said quietly but he remained deadpan, releasing her hand.

'*Adios*, Barbara—'

'Why! Isn't that Amelia Corey just getting out of the coach. Yes! I believe so.'

Nevada grunted, moving to tie the reins of his chestnut to the tailgate of the stagecoach. He had arranged previously with the booking clerk to take it along, and had paid an extra dollar for the privilege.

Then he felt himself stiffen as Amelia lifted her veil – black, matching her dress, still in mourning for Linus Ketchum – saw him, and came across, her face lighting up in a wide smile.

'Oh, Nevada! How very glad I am to see you!' He frowned as she stopped in front of him. 'Did you think I'd forgotten about you?'

A bit nonplussed, Nevada waited, mighty leery now. Barbara smiled hesitantly but Amelia's eyes were only for Nevada. The smile remained as she spoke and her eyes glittered.

'I believe I am carrying Jim Corey's son, Nevada. I hope so, anyway, because I want him to be just like his father! But no matter, if it's a girl, I will bring her up just the same. And when I have other children, they, too, will be brought up just like their brothers or sisters.'

Suddenly the smile vanished, and she said viciously: 'You see, I intend to teach them all to *hate, with all their being, the name of Nevada Hawk!* Then they will teach their children to hate you, too, and they, in turn, will pass it on to *their* families!' She laughed but it was more a humorless cackle than anything. 'Ah! I see that has shaken you some! I'm glad! I told you once I was a patient woman and could wait for my revenge. I haven't finished with you yet!' She stepped closer and he involuntarily took a step back, very uneasy about all this.

Her hand grabbed his arm in the sling and she squeezed very hard, obviously hoping to cause him pain. But his face registered nothing. Her mouth curled in scorn and hatred. 'I hope you marry and have a family of your own, Nevada – I truly do. Because every minute of every day for the rest of your life you're going to have to worry about them! Because *my* family will have as their sole goal in life, the destruction of yours! You will never know when they will strike. *You'll* be all right, safe and sound – I don't want any harm to come to you. Or your wife, because I know you'll suffer just watching her anguish as she loses her children one by one—'

'Get the hell away from me!' said Nevada in a choking voice, fighting not to strangle this crazy woman.

Amelia smiled that cold smile. 'We'll find you wherever you go. Your family will never know peace. One by one they'll die. I want to bring you suffering like you've brought me – you dirty, murdering son of a *bitch*!'

She slapped him brutally across the face and he felt tears of pain squeeze from his eyes. When he could see properly again, she was walking away down the boardwalk, the crowd opening out for her.

'Oh, my God, Nevada!' gasped Barbara. 'I-I feel sick. What will you do?'

'What is there to do?' he answered. 'The only way to stop her would be to kill her.'

'And you won't do that. You're not that kind of man. What a dreadful future she has just outlined for you!'

He moved towards the coach where the driver, impatient to be on his way again to Santa Fe, was holding the door open. He spoke just before stepping inside. 'Never known anyone yet who could *really* predict the future,' he said. 'No one can tell what'll happen.'

He touched a hand to his hatbrim and stepped on board. With a tear in her eye Barbara waved as the stage pulled away in a cloud of dust. 'She could die in childbirth – she's not a well woman!' she thought. 'Or the baby could be – stillborn. . . .' She stopped thinking such things, turned away. It was all too ugly to even contemplate. *It was Nevada's problem, anyway. She'd squeezed all the use she could out of him. And it had worked out very well – for her. Bad luck for him, but – he'd really brought it all on himself. Hadn't he?*

Yes, of course, he had. Well, she had plenty to think about in regard to Broken T's future. That would be much more pleasant than worrying about a crazy woman like Amelia Corey.

Staring out of the window as the stagecoach clattered down Main, Nevada watched the town slide by. He glimpsed Amelia again, standing on a street corner, staring bleakly. Their eyes locked briefly. Then she slid past and the stage rocked across the wooden bridge spanning the narrow creek and began the long, slow climb up into the hills.

'I never did plan on marrying again, anyway,' Nevada murmured. The drummer beside him looked at him sharply, but refrained from making any kind of comment.

As the stage slowed for the winding trail around the mesa, Nevada smiled thinly. *That was one way of beating Amelia Corey's threats. Never marry. Never have any children she could reach out for in her demented quest for vengeance. . . . Yeah, he could beat her that way.*

But it was going to be one hell of a lonely life.

Just him – and his memories of Ellie.

Hell, he could live with that! They were good memories and could keep a man company for a long, long time.